THE DEBT

INSTALLMENT THREE

THE DEBT

Installment One: Catch the Zolt

Installment Two: Turn off the Lights

Installment Three: Bring Back Cerberus

Installment Four: Fetch the Treasure Hunter

Installment Five: Yamashita's Gold

Installment Six: Take a Life

THE DEBT

INSTALLMENT THREE

BRING BACK CERBERUS

PHILLIP GWYNNE

Kane Miller

A DIVISION OF EDC PUBLISHING

First American Edition 2014
Kane Miller, A Division of EDC Publishing

Copyright © Phillip Gwynne 2013
Cover and internal design copyright © Allen & Unwin 2013
Cover and text design by Natalie Winter
Cover photography: (boy) by Alan Richardson Photography,
    model: Nicolai Laptev; (runner) © Dex Image/Corbis

For information contact:
Kane Miller, A Division of EDC Publishing
PO Box 470663
Tulsa, OK 74147-0663

www.kanemiller.com
www.edcpub.com
www.usbornebooksandmore.com

Library of Congress Control Number: 2013953412

Printed and bound in the United States of America
1 2 3 4 5 6 7 8 9 10
ISBN: 978-1-61067-305-1

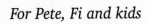

For Pete, Fi and kids

DISCIPULE, CARO MORTUA ES

As I walked through the school gates I could see Dr. Chakrabarty coming out of the library, a stack of books under one arm, a folded-up newspaper in his other hand. Because I hadn't seen him for a while I'd figured he'd retired, or he'd died, or he'd found some other sneaky way to get out of teaching classics. Let's face it, Ancient Greek and Latin weren't exactly hot-ticket items at Coast Boys Grammar. Now if he'd taught How to Succeed at Business When Your Family Is Already Filthy Rich, or Advanced Surfing: Beyond Being Stoked, then I'm sure his services would have been in more demand. As it was, he seemed to spend most of his time shuffling between the library and his office, which was situated in the oldest part of the school, the stone building officially called the Cloisters but, since Harry Potter, more commonly known as Hogwarts (or Warthogs if you were the amusing type).

I took out my iPhone, scrolled down to that text message. *Discipule, caro mortua es.*

When I'd first received it, I'd tried to work out what it meant. But all Google Translate had come up with was "Disciple, flesh of a dead Are." And BabelFish didn't even have a Latin-to-English option. I'd just ignored it. And nothing bad had happened to me, so I'd kept ignoring it. But seeing Dr. Chakrabarty shuffling out of the library like that made me think that I could show it to him, see what he made of it.

As I approached him I smelled a musty smell. Whether it emanated from him or the stack of books he was carrying under his arm, I wasn't sure. I quickly scanned their titles, which were all to do with ancient Rome or ancient Greece, except for one book, newer than the others, called *The Carbon Debate*.

"Hello, Dr. Chakrabarty," I said.

"No need to yell, son," he said, looking at me from under the shaggiest eyebrows the world has ever known. "I may be ancient, but there's nothing wrong with my hearing."

"Sorry, sir," I said, lowering my voice several decibels.

"What did you say?" he said.

"I said 'I'm sorry,'" I said, raising my voice again.

This volume seemed to work because he said, "And what's your name, young man?"

"Dominic," I said. "Dominic Silvagni."

"So how can I help you, Dominic?"

But before I had a chance to say anything he said, "*Arti undis uectandi deditus sum.*"

"Sorry?" I said.

"That's Latin for 'Live to surf.' It seems the most popular translation I am asked for these days. I believe one of our more forgetful students even had it tattooed on his buttocks. Or *Natus ut rotis caligaribus vectus essem.*"

"Born to skate?" I said.

"Very good!" he said. "You obviously have the makings of a classics scholar."

Of course I thought he was being sarcastic, first weapon of choice for most teachers since corporal punishment had been outlawed, but when I looked at his face I changed my mind – no, he was fair dinkum.

But I guess poor old Dr. Chakrabarty must've been pretty desperate for students because I didn't know anybody who took one of his subjects, not even Peter Eisinger, and Peter Eisinger takes all the weird and wacky subjects. In fact, that's who Peter Eisinger is: the kid who takes all the weird and wacky subjects.

"Actually I'm probably more of a runner than a scholar," I said.

"A runner?" he replied. "Our very own Pheidippides."

"Who?" I said.

And then Dr. Chakrabarty was off like a runner himself, a verbal one.

"In 490 BC an Athenian herald by the name of Pheidippides was sent to Sparta to request help when the Persians landed in Marathon in Greece," he said.

"There was actually a place called Marathon?"

"Most certainly," said Dr. Chakrabarty. "According to Herodotus, Pheidippides ran the two hundred and forty kilometers in two days. He then ran the forty kilometers from the battlefield at Marathon to Athens to announce a Greek victory with the single word '*Nenikékamen.*' We have won!"

It was pretty cool hearing Dr. Chakrabarty talk about old Pheidippides like that, and I sort of wished I'd approached him and his eyebrows before.

"So what happened to him then?" I asked, ready to be wowed by further extraordinary running feats.

"He dropped dead," said Dr. Chakrabarty.

Dropped dead?

"From exhaustion."

Even more reason to stick to middle distance running, I thought.

Dr. Chakrabarty was then off again, talking about how old Pheidippides had supposedly met the god Pan on Mount Parthenium, how it was actually Pan who helped the Greeks win the battle of Marathon by causing the opposing soldiers to flee in a frenzy of fear.

"And that is where we get the word 'panic.'" said Dr. Chakrabarty. "From the god Pan."

Maybe Peter Eisinger had it right, I thought. Weird and wacky was the way to go.

Still, the text message, the one I'd ignored, was now blinking brightly in my head. So when Dr. Chakrabarty stopped to draw breath I interrupted. "Could you translate something for me?"

"Latin?"

"I think so," I said, holding up my iPhone with the text message on it.

"Eyesight's not what it used to be," he said, holding out the newspaper. "Take this so I can have a closer look."

I swapped my iPhone for his newspaper.

As Dr. Chakrabarty considered what was on the screen my eyes were drawn to the newspaper, to the half-finished cryptic crossword.

I scanned the clues: *Outlaw leader managing money* and *Initially amiable person eats primate.*

Really, how could anybody make sense of that?

Eventually Dr. Chakrabarty said, "This is the iPhone 5, right?"

"Yes," I said.

"Very nice. I wonder if I can upgrade on my plan?"

"Who you with?"

"Virgin."

"I think they've got, like, this humungous waiting list."

"Then what are your thoughts on these new Styxx phones? They seem to be quite popular now."

"Mostly with nerds," I said.

He then made a long and complicated joke – well, I think it was a joke – about virgins and waiting lists, which I didn't get at all.

When he'd finished I said, "The message?"

"Ah yes, the message."

Again he turned his attention to my phone. As he read, his shaggy eyebrows moved up and down, in and out, up and down. Watching them was sort of mesmerizing, like watching two sheep doing ballet, and when he spoke again the urgency in his voice startled me. "Who sent you this?"

"I'm not sure."

"It's quite a lovely effort," he said.

"But what does it mean?" I said as the bell went and students immediately started making for their respective classrooms.

"You're not in any sort of trouble, are you?"

There was no way I was going to tell him about The Debt, about the ancient family obligation I had inherited. I wasn't going to tell him about the letters my own father had branded onto the inside of my thigh. How I couldn't go anywhere near a barbecue now, how the smell of searing meat made me feel instantly nauseous. I wasn't going to tell him how they'd taken "a pound of flesh" from my grandfather, how they'd amputated his leg. And how they'd do the same to me if I didn't pay the next four installments. I wasn't going to tell him how I'd captured the Zolt, how I'd turned off all the lights on the Gold Coast during Earth Hour. How the cops were now on my trail. I wasn't going to tell Dr. Chakrabarty and his shaggy sheep eyebrows any of that stuff.

He repeated his question, his eyes searching my face. "You're not in any sort of trouble, are you?"

"No, sir," I said.

The sheep did some more ballet and then he returned to the text.

"It's a threat," he said. "And not a very pleasant one."

"A threat?" I repeated.

"The best translation I can give is 'Schoolboy, you are dead meat.'"

"Whoa!"

I felt a chill, a shiver that started at my toes and traveled all the way up my spine and then all the way back down again.

Schoolboy, you are dead meat.

I'd received the text just after I'd repaid the second installment, after I'd turned off the lights, after I'd done everything The Debt had asked of me. How could I then be dead meat?

No matter how you looked at it, it wasn't fair!

YOU AIN'T NOTHING BUT A HOUND DE VILLIERS

After school we had training.

"Before we start," said Coach Sheeds to the assembled runners, "let's give Rashid, Bevan and Dom a big hand for qualifying for the national titles."

Rashid, Bevan and Dom got a hand, but it wasn't exactly "big."

And I couldn't blame my fellow athletes for holding back a bit in the hand department, because the way we'd qualified had been pretty lame.

When the race was first run there'd been the lights-out fiasco.

And then, in the rerun, the top four positions had again been taken by the imported Kenyans.

Though, weirdly enough, in a time that was about five seconds less than my PB.

It was almost like we hadn't even competed; we'd figured that they'd deserved to win because they'd been leading when the lights had gone out.

But then an official from Townsville by the name of Marge Jenkins had done some serious digging and found out that the Kenyans weren't on the right type of visa.

After they were disqualified the next four runners, including Rashid, Bevan Milne and yours truly, became eligible to compete in the nationals.

See what I mean, hardly big-hand material.

"Okay, let's have ten four hundreds at three-quarter pace," said Coach Sheeds.

There were a few groans, but there were always a few groans.

Coach Sheeds could say, "Let's lie in a hammock for the next ten minutes," and somebody would be sure to say, "Aw, do we have to?"

As I got into the first four hundred I realized how good it felt to be running again, to be part of the world I knew, and loved, best. Concentrating on the here and the now, not letting the past or the future intrude, getting everything – legs, arms, breath, brain – working in unison.

"Looking good, Dom," Coach Sheeds yelled out to me.

Feeling good, too, Coach, I thought, a sudden wave of elation lifting me up: lame qualification or not, I was so ready to run the race of my life in Sydney.

After the final rep Coach Sheeds called us in.

As we gathered by the long jump pit again she handed out an itinerary to each of us.

"Study this," she said.

I read it quickly: we were to meet Saturday at lunchtime, travel to Sydney on a bus and stay the night at a hotel. The next day we'd attend the meet and then return that evening.

Mom and Dad were making a big deal about this meet: they were flying down and staying at a hotel on the harbor. And I guess if I made enough fuss – or Dad, major benefactor of my school, made enough fuss – I could've gone with them.

But I was actually looking forward to the bus trip.

Yes, Bevan Milne's farts would get louder, smellier, and wetter as the trip went on. And Rashid would tell the same unfunny joke about a thousand times. And Coach Sheeds would insist on the world's dorkiest sing-along. But it would be fun, I knew it would.

My attention wandered then. It was a typical Gold Coast sky: high, blue and cloudless, but in one corner was a glint of white as a light plane wobbled its way southwards.

Although it hadn't been so long ago that I'd been in such a plane myself, a plane piloted by Otto

Zolton-Bander, the so-called Facebook Bandit, that memory had already acquired a sort of cinematic quality, as if it hadn't actually happened to me.

I knew this was an illusion, however, because it had happened to me, and it would happen again. Not the plane thing, necessarily, but another installment. And it could be anytime soon.

The ClamTop could swing open tonight and there it would be. Or that pathetic treadmill could start talking to me again with its California voice.

"Has anybody got any questions?" said Coach Sheeds.

There were no questions, so Coach Sheeds said, "Get in here and listen up."

Hakuna Matata time.

"Every morning in Africa, a gazelle wakes up, knowing it must run faster than the fastest lion or it will be killed. Every morning in Africa, a lion wakes up, knowing it must run faster than the slowest gazelle or it will starve," she said.

We crowded in closer, our voices joining Coach Sheeds's.

"So it doesn't matter whether you're a lion or a gazelle because when the sun comes up, you better be bloody well running."

Hakuna Matata!

"And don't forget training tomorrow, either!" said Coach Sheeds.

My civics teacher, Mr. Ryan, was waiting outside the locker room, dressed, as usual, in spotless chinos and a spotless blue linen shirt. There was some debate among us students as to whether it was the same chinos and blue shirt, washed, dried and ironed at the end of each school day, or whether Mr. Ryan's wardrobe contained multiple copies of the same outfit.

"You guys ready for the big day?" he said.

"Sure," I said.

"It's going to be tough," I added.

"The nationals are always tough," said Mr. Ryan. "Often tougher than running internationally."

He knew what he was talking about, too: in the eighties, when he was a student at this school, he'd been a champion cross-country runner, and he still held the record for 8 kilometers.

We talked about the titles for a while before he said, "About that other business, Dom."

That other business, I assumed, was the fact that the police had been pestering me ever since all the lights in the Gold Coast went out during Earth Hour.

The other business Mr. Ryan became involved in because he was once a lawyer.

"Yes," I said, my heart going one way, my guts the other. They, like me, were thinking the worst: that finally the authorities had proof it was me.

"It seems that the police aren't so interested in Diablo anymore."

"That's great," I said, heart and guts returning to their customary positions.

"Yes, it is," he said. "But your name has somehow come up in regards to another, unrelated, matter."

Mr. Ryan was starting to sound less and less like the chino-clad teacher he was and more and more like the lawyer he used to be.

But not just that, he was sounding like a lawyer who had some serious connections.

"You've heard of Otto Zolton-Bander?"

My first instinct was to say no, to deny absolutely all knowledge of Otto Zolton-Bander, but that would be silly because everybody had heard of the Zolt.

"Yes, of course," I said. "But isn't he, like, dead now?"

"Well, that's what they're saying. But it's all very confusing. Anyway, they seem to think that you're somehow connected to him. There's even some suggestion that you were in the plane with him when he landed in Ibbotson Reserve."

"That's crazy," I said, readying myself for some more involuntary movement from my bodily parts.

But they remained where they were.

"I was running in a race on Reverie Island when all that happened," I said, this lie sliding easily off my tongue.

It occurred to me that, if nothing else, The Debt had taught me how to lie. Hey, if my running career came to nothing, maybe I could tell porkies for Australia instead.

"You were?" said Mr. Ryan, his eyes searching mine. "So you've got yourself a pretty good alibi, then?"

So-so, I thought. But I did have a grandfather who'd probably be willing to stretch the truth just a bit.

"An excellent alibi," I said.

"That's great news," said Mr. Ryan, slapping me on the back.

"So have you got an invoice or anything?" I said. "So my dad can pay you for all this work you've done?"

Mr. Ryan threw up his arms. "Don't be silly, Dom. It's actually quite fun being involved with the law again. Much more fun than when I actually was a lawyer."

We said our good-byes, I got changed, and as I made my way home I couldn't help thinking about Mr. Ryan.

He was obviously a really good lawyer who got a big kick out of the law. Seriously, would you give that up for chinos and a classroom of smart-aleck kids?

As I walked past a park where a couple of ducks, wings spread, were sunning themselves by a pond, a black Hummer pulled up onto the footpath right in front of me. The window wound down, and I was looking into the scary blue eyes of Hound de Villiers, Private Investigator.

I could've made a run for it across the park, and I probably had a good chance of getting away, but I figured that was the dumb option. Hound would find me again for sure. Because finding people is what Hound does for a living.

And Hummers weren't cheap: he obviously made a very good living.

Hound kept staring at me with those scary blue eyes.

Say something, I told myself.

Anything to break the ice, I told myself.

"That's come up really well," I said, pointing to the side of the Hummer.

The last time I'd seen it, it'd just been rammed by a Mercedes driven by Otto Zolton-Bander and hadn't looked so straight.

"Tell me this: if I wasted you right now, who would actually care?" said Hound.

Was Hound capable of wasting somebody in broad daylight like this?

No, probably not, but he was still a seriously big, seriously scary dude. His office was full of all these photos of him with all these guns and he'd whacked me once, right across the head, and my ears had rung for hours after.

"I mean, who would care?" said Hound.

"Quite a few people, actually," I said, sliding my iPhone out of my pocket and snapping a photo of Hound. "The person I just sent that photo to, for example," I continued. "They'd care. Probably care enough to take it to the cops if I didn't get home tonight."

Hound stared at me for a while longer with his scary blue eyes, before he said, "So where is he?"

"By he, I assume you are referring to Otto Zolton-Bander?" I said.

"You are really starting to get on my nerves, punk," said Hound.

"He's dead," I said quickly. "Don't you watch Fox News?"

I could tell from the look on Hound's face that he didn't believe the Zolt was dead. And I didn't really blame him, because I was pretty sure he wasn't dead either. Unless somebody else had taken it upon themselves to fly over Halcyon Grove in a light plane and deposit a fake Double Eagle coin into our pool.

"Where is he?" he repeated.

"I seriously don't know," I said.

Hound thought about this for a while before he said, "You willing to take a polygraph?"

"A lie detector test?" I said

"Exactly," said Hound. "My office, tomorrow, five."

"Okay, I'll be there," I said, though I had absolutely no intention of turning up at his office tomorrow at five. Firstly I had training, and secondly this had to be some sort of trap.

The window wound up and the Hummer reversed off the footpath, and bullied its way back into the stream of traffic.

VIRTUALLY IMOGEN

I knew it was wrong. I knew it was immoral. I knew it was unethical. I knew it was … Okay, you name it, I knew it.

But I couldn't help myself, because I was desperate to see her, even if that "her" was the digital "her."

Ever since I'd confessed to Imogen that it was me who had set fire to the Jazys' pool she hadn't talked to me. Hadn't even acknowledged me.

It was like I was invisible, like I was made of air, a total non-being.

So after I locked my bedroom door, I sat in front of ClamTop.

"Open," I said, and it immediately opened.

"Networks," I commanded, and again it responded, bringing up all the networks in the area.

I knew she was home because earlier, when I'd walked past, I'd seen her shape at her bedroom window.

But that still didn't mean their network would be up.

It was, though.

My excitement increasing exponentially, I opened HAVILLAND and cloned SYLVIA, Imogen's computer.

There was nothing open, not an application, not a program, not a widget. All the icons were lined up on her desktop, perfect rows and perfect columns.

She wasn't there, and that excitement I'd generated became disappointment.

"Come on, you little turds!" I yelled at the motionless icons. "Do something!"

But the little turds did absolutely nothing.

I did notice something, however: she'd changed her wallpaper; it was now a picture of her missing father. Taken from a newspaper, it showed him, arms thrust triumphantly into the air, celebrating a win in some sort of election. Mrs. Havilland was by his side, looking very beautiful, very sophisticated. And she was holding the hand of a little girl who had huge eyes and lots of curly blond hair. Imogen.

Behind these three were a whole lot of other happy-looking people who I guessed were members of Mr. Havilland's election campaign. Although they weren't quite in focus, one of them looked familiar somehow.

My eyes flicked between the person in the photo – who was it? – and the motionless icons.

Come on, you little turds, do something.

The real Imogen wouldn't talk to me and now it seemed the virtual one wouldn't either.

I waited for five, ten, twenty minutes and nothing changed, the icons remaining motionless, the person in the photo unrecognized.

Thirty minutes, forty minutes.

Where could she be?

And immediately a whole lot of explanations presented themselves, each one seemingly more plausible than the one before: Imogen was with Tristan, Imogen was with somebody else even more not-okay than Tristan, Imogen had choked on a Chupa Chup and was now lying dead on her bedroom floor.

After an hour I decided that enough was enough, that I should de-clone Imogen's computer, that I should log off and go do something more useful with my life.

Okay, that's what I decided to do, but that's not what I did.

I opened Windows Mail. Yes, it was wrong, it was immoral, it was unethical, but it's what I did. Because I was opening a clone of her program and not the real thing I thought it wouldn't download any new mail.

I was wrong.

Bang! Bang! Bang! Bang! Four new messages.

I started to panic. What if Imogen found out that I'd been tampering with her email? But again I remembered what Dr. Chakrabarty had told me: panic was just something invented by the god Pan to scare a few soldiers.

I stopped panicking.

And when I did I soon realized that there was really nothing to worry about, because computers do screwy stuff all the time. There are viruses, there's malware, there are software bugs, there are so many excuses for them when they go mental. And there was no way Imogen would know it was me anyway, because ClamTop was the stealthiest of stealth bombers.

Now that that was out of the way, I couldn't help but look at these newly arrived emails. Especially since the first one was from Fiends of the Earth.

Fiends of the Earth!

Immediately my brain started playing "Construct the Conspiracy."

Imogen had tipped off Fiends of the Earth about me, Imogen was on their payroll, Imogen was the infamous Dr. E.!

But then I remembered that it was Imogen who had told me about Fiends of the Earth in the first place. And, committed greenie that she was, it wouldn't be surprising if she received regular emails from them. The same way she received regular emails from Greenpeace, Sea Shepherd and Save the Whales.

When I opened it, I soon realized that I was right, because it was a pretty generic sort of correspondence thanking the recipient for their continued support, without which they wouldn't be able to blah blah blah.

I was just about to stop reading but two words – *Diablo* and *Bay* – further on in the email grabbed my eye, so I skipped to that bit.

The ongoing campaign to have the Diablo Bay Nuclear Power Station decommissioned has been giving a boost after an internal document aired on Internet site Wikileaks indicated that the recent total blackout on the Gold Coast during Earth Hour was caused by a cyber-attack on their computer system.

Wow, Diablo Bay Nuclear Power Station decommissioned because of me!

I had this power rush, like I'd just knocked back several Red Bulls.

I kept reading.

The campaign has recently received a generous donation from an anonymous source.

Then there was more blah blah blah, which I skimmed through.

Right at the end Max Denton of the Scuba Divers Association said that *decommissioning Diablo Bay and opening up the riches of the adjacent coastline*

once again for recreational use would be welcomed by all in the diving community.

The next email was from Tristan.

I opened it thinking the worst, that all the sympathy Imogen had stored for the comatose Tristan had caused her to throw herself at the non-comatose Tristan, that Tristan and Imogen were an item.

But I wasn't just thinking the worst, it was almost as if I was hoping the worst, because then I could be angry, I could be outraged, I could be aggrieved.

dear im, the email began and already I was angry – who said he could call Imogen that? It was my name for her.

The email continued, *the dr said that because I'm not getting better I can't go to school until next term so tks so much for all the dvds.*

Okay, that wasn't so bad – in fact, I almost felt sorry for Tristan, a) because he had to stay home, and b) because Imogen had some really crap DVDs.

I kept reading.

I reckon you're being a bit hard on dom. it wasn't his fault i spent so much time in la-la-land just a couple of boys mucking about in boats. ☺ ☺

Geez – what was happening here?

Could this be the same Tristan who had punched me in the guts?

Instead of outraged, I was sort of touched. Instead

of angry, I was grateful. And "aggrieved" could go back into the online thesaurus where I'd found it.

talk to you soon im tristan

Even the *im* didn't rile me as much second time around.

I closed Windows Mail and there it was again, the photo taken after the election win.

And then it occurred to me: how to get Imogen back onside. How to build that bridge over the abyss between us.

If I found out who these people were, then hopefully she would start talking to me. Hopefully.

And something else occurred to me: finding who these people were was Private Investigating 101.

So maybe I would turn up at the meeting/trap with Hound de Villiers tomorrow, after all.

LIES

"I have to go now," I said to Coach Sheeds in the middle of training after school on Tuesday.

"Now?" she said.

"That's right, now," I said.

"You are kidding me!"

"No."

Coach Sheeds looked up and down the track as if to make sure no other runner could hear what she was about to say.

Then she looked me in the eye and said, "You could go to Rome, Dom."

I knew exactly what that meant: if I placed in the top four runners at the nationals and made the Australian team, then I would go to the World Youth Games in Rome later in the year.

This was a very un-Coach-Sheeds-like thing to say because she didn't play favorites, treating all her runners equally. We were all gazelles. All lions.

She continued, "Now that you've got your mind back on the job, you could do it."

I'm pretty sure I blushed. *Ohmigod, Coach Sheeds thinks I can do it!*

"But only if you keep your bloody mind on the job," she said.

Maybe I should keep to my original plan and blow Hound de Villiers off, I thought. But that image popped up in my mind again, the one that had been popping up all day: Hound helping me build a bridge across the abyss that separated me from Imogen.

"I'm sorry, Coach," I said, and I really was sorry.

Okay, Gus was probably right: she wasn't exactly the best coach in the business, but she was officially my coach at school. The last thing I wanted to do was let her down.

"But I really have to go," I said, and I really did have to go.

Again that look from Coach Sheeds, up and down the track, before she leaned in closer.

"This is in the vault, okay?"

I nodded.

"I was once in exactly the same situation as you, Dom. The same age as you. Had the world at my feet. Everybody said I was cert to go to Helsinki for the World Youth Games."

"What happened?" I said.

27

I knew Coach Sheeds had been an elite runner but I didn't know this.

"I got distracted. You don't have to know the details, but I got distracted. And that, really, was the end of my career. Sure, I kept on running, but it wasn't the same after that because nobody took me seriously as an athlete." Coach paused as if something had just occurred to her before she said, "Not even me."

She smiled at me. "And do you know what, there's not a day that passes when I don't think about it, when I don't imagine what I could've bloody well been."

"But you're our coach!" I said, and as soon as I did I realized it was exactly the wrong thing to say.

Because everybody knows that saying: Those who can, do. And those who can't, coach.

And now it was like both of us were standing in a knee-deep puddle of failure, of disappointment, of what-could've-bloody-well-been.

Again that image: me and Hound building a bridge, and I said, "I have to go."

I left Coach standing there by herself, in the puddle.

The first three taxis I hailed refused to take me to the Block.

"Too dangerous," said the first.

"Are you crazy?" said the second.

"God help you," said the third, even when I offered to double the fare.

So I had no choice: I found Luiz Antonio's card in my wallet, called his mobile number.

"I'm on another call," he said. "I'll be there in fifteen minutes."

"Okay," I said.

Twenty minutes later he pulled up and I got into the front seat.

"Guess who was sitting right where you're sitting?" said Luiz Antonio, and the excitement emanating from him was almost palpable.

"Um, Hicham El Guerrouj?" I said.

"Who?"

"Never mind," I said. "I give up, who was sitting right where I'm sitting?"

"Silva da Silva!" he said, a note of triumph in his voice. "In my taxi!"

"The UFC fighter?" I said, and I had this brush-with-fame feeling, like that time when I bodysurfed the same wave as Ian Thorpe and his ginormous feet at Burleigh Heads.

"So you know him?"

"Yes," I said, though the truth was that I hardly knew anything about him. It was just that a lot of kids at school were into UFC, especially Bevan Milne, and when they talked about the fighters, Silva da Silva was the one who seemed to get mentioned the most.

"He's from Rio, he's a Carioca like me," said Luiz Antonio. "And next week he fights for the world championship, here in the Gold Coast!"

I'd seen UFC a few times on television, and though I could appreciate that they were incredibly fit athletes, that was about as far as my appreciation went. The biffing and banging wasn't too bad, but when they started wrestling, getting close and sweaty on the mat, my hand reached for the remote.

As we drove on, weaving through the afternoon traffic, Luiz Antonio continued talking about Silva da Silva and the UFC. It was pretty obvious that he knew a lot about both, and I was starting to buy into his enthusiasm. When we pulled up outside the Cash Converters, I didn't really want to get out. I wanted Luiz Antonio to keep driving around and around, talking in his lilting voice, but I knew I had no choice but to meet Hound de Villiers.

When I went to pay the fare Luiz Antonio said, "Fix me up at the end."

"So you're going to wait?"

Luiz Antonio held out his hands out as if to say, *What do you expect?*

It felt pretty reassuring to know that he'd be here, waiting. Especially when I saw the same bunch of desperadoes as last time hanging outside the front of Cash Converters, including the one in the red bandana, the one who'd used me and Tristan for target practice at Reverie Island.

But I also couldn't help wondering who Luiz Antonio was.

Obviously, he was on somebody's payroll, but whose exactly?

I thanked him and made my way to the entrance, to the desperadoes. Head down, I pushed through them, dispensing with the usual "Excuse me," keen to get inside in case Red Bandana recognized me.

Once inside I ignored the front counter and made for the stairs, taking them two at a time until I reached the first floor.

Just as I was about to knock on the door to Hound's office, it opened and a man, similar in size and scariness to Hound, came out.

He looked up at me, but obviously wasn't impressed with what he saw because he looked straight back down again and kept walking.

"Hi," I said to Hound after I'd entered his office.

He indicated a chair: *sit down*.

"So you reckon you don't know where Zolton-Bander is?" he said from behind his desk.

"I wouldn't have a clue," I said. "And like I said, I'm willing to take a lie detector test to prove it."

"Great!" he said, opening a drawer in his desk, rummaging inside.

I scanned the walls, taking in all the photos of Hound de Villiers toting firearms of various sizes and destructive power.

A photo I hadn't noticed before caught my attention; in this one Hound was with a person, rather than an AK-47, his arm around their shoulder. And it wasn't any old person, it was the Treasure Hunter himself: E. Lee Marx.

"You know E. Lee Marx?" I said.

"We go way back," said Hound. "Back to Army days."

"He's South African?"

Hound smiled. "Yes, not something he likes to broadcast, though. Not television-friendly enough."

"So you saw *The Treasure Hunter*?" I said.

"Load of old bollocks," he said. "I told him that when I was talking to him last week."

"You talk to him?" I said.

"Every now and then. Like I said: we go way back, us two." He brought out an iPod-sized device from the drawer. "Hold out your hand."

He strapped the device to the wrist of my right hand. Two wires led to adhesive sensor pads which he stuck to my palm, and a third wire ended in a pulse meter which he clipped onto the end of my forefinger.

He plugged the device into the USB port of the iMac on his desk.

"Okay, you ready?" he said.

I nodded.

"Is your name Dom Silvagni?" he asked.

"Yes," I answered.

"Do you have three heads?"

"No," I answered.

If only exams at school were so easy.

Now that he'd calibrated the machine he said, "Do you know where Otto Zolton-Bander is?"

"No," I replied, confident that the device would tell him that I wasn't lying.

"Okay, then," he said, reading from the screen, "maybe you don't know where he is, after all."

I smiled at him and his excellent machine.

"Okay, let's try this one. Did you hack into the Diablo Bay Nuclear Power Station's computer system?"

I'd suspected a trap, but I hadn't expected it to be sprung so quickly.

"Who told you that?" I said.

"Just because I got no respect for the cops, doesn't mean I don't have a couple on the payroll," said Hound. "Did you hack into the Diablo Bay Nuclear Power Station's computer system?"

"Antidisestablishmentarianism," I said.

"What in the blazes is that?"

Though I was aware of all those photos of Hound with all those guns, though I could remember just

33

how easily he'd zinged my head, I was also aware that I couldn't just be the scared little guy – I had to show some guts, some major 'tude.

"I believe it's the longest word in the English language," I said.

I unclipped the pulse meter from my finger, removed the sensors from my palm and, yanking it loose from my wrist, tossed the lie detector onto his desk.

As I did, the cover of the battery compartment fell off. There were no batteries inside.

I looked at Hound and he had this sort of guilty look on his face, like a small kid who has been caught doing something wrong.

"Why are you so desperate to blackmail me?" I said.

"Tell me how you did it, how you hacked into their system. That place has a triple-A security rating."

"Antidisestablishmentarianism," I said.

"So why'd you want to turn off the city lights like that? You some sort of hippie, are you, Dom? Some sort of dope-smoking, tree-hugging, muesli-eating freak?"

I gave my standard answer.

I could see the color rising in Hound's face – it was probably time to lose the "antidisestablishmentarianism" thing.

"What do you want me for anyway?" I said.

"I want you to help people help themselves."

My face must've done a pretty good job of conveying my incomprehension, because Hound immediately launched into an explanation. "Most of my clients are good people, Dom. Good people but they've just strayed from the path. I see it as my job to get them back on the path. Sometimes they forget that. They forget their court appointments. They forget their repayments. They forget their debts. So I have to find them. Remind them. Get them back on that path."

"I still don't see how I can help," I said.

"It's a technological world we live in, Dom. Everything's interconnected. I employ the best I can find, but I'm just not sure Guzman's got your skill set."

"Guzman?" I said.

"My tech guy."

"So why didn't you just ask me if I wanted a job like any normal person?" I said.

Hound shrugged and said, "Do you want a job like any normal person?"

"Not really," I said. "But maybe we could arrange some sort of contra deal."

"Contra deals are good," said Hound. "Keep the taxman's big nose well out of it. What did you have in mind?"

I began telling him what I had in mind and Hound leaned back in his chair, hands clasped behind his head.

When I'd finished Hound said, "I reckon we might just have ourselves a deal, Youngblood."

"Youngblood?" I said.

"Youngblood," he said. "From now on you're Youngblood."

NITMICK

Wednesday, and there was still no sign of The Debt, of the next installment.

Stop thinking about it, I ordered myself. But you can't tell yourself to stop thinking about something, it just makes you think about it more.

But what you can do is think about something else. Like the race. Like running.

During math, while the teacher droned on about Pythagoras and his theorem, I did some excellent arithmetic on my calculator. My PB for the 1500 meters was 4.01.4 minutes, which was an average speed of 6.21 m/sec. My PB for the 800 meters was 1.57.2 minutes, which was an average speed of 6.83 m/sec. So if I could maintain my 800 speed for the entire 1500 meters I'd do it in 3.39.6 minutes! In 1957, 3.39.6 would've broken the men's world record.

During biology, while the teacher droned on about the carbon cycle, I thought about lactic acid. During strenuous exercise the body derives energy by breaking down stored glucose. Which causes production of a substance called pyruvate. Which, in the absence of oxygen, is converted to lactate. Which causes acidity in the muscles. And that horrible thighs-on-fire sensation I always got in the third lap.

During English, while Mr. McFarlane droned on about the ancient Japanese poetic form known as the haiku, I actually listened to what he had to say. And when he gave us ten minutes to compose our own haiku, I actually put pen to paper.

"And do you have something wonderful to share with us today, Dom?" he said, not even bothering to hide the sarcasm in his voice.

"I do, actually," I said, standing up.

Adopting my best poetry declaiming voice, I read from the piece of paper:

"Run fast as I can
Running running running fast
As fast as I can."

Just as I finished, and the first snickers started, there was a knock on the door.

The red-haired kid entered, the one who used to have an neck brace but was now sporting an eye patch. He said something to Mr. McFarlane.

"Dom," said Mr. McFarlane, his eyes falling on me. "You're to report to the front office immediately."

I got up, conscious that all my classmates were looking at me thinking, "What trouble is Silvagni in this time?"

And maybe some of them were also thinking, "Why does Silvagni, former Goody Two-shoes, always seem to be getting into trouble these days?"

"Do you know what it's about?" I asked the red-haired kid with the eye patch as we hurried back along the corridor.

"Hey, hombre, I'm only the messenger," he said.

"So what happened to your eye?" I said.

"Don't even begin to ask," he replied.

When we got to the office, Mr. Iharos, the vice principal, was waiting for us.

He was definitely not wearing a you're-in-big-trouble look, so I relaxed a bit.

But not for long.

If I wasn't in trouble, who was? At Grammar they don't just drag kids out of class for any old reason.

"Is my family okay?" I asked.

"Dom, that's something you better ask your uncle," said Mr. Iharos.

Before I could utter "My uncle?" or "What uncle?" my uncle stepped out from Mr. Iharos's office.

My uncle was wearing an expensive suit. An expensive watch. My uncle really looked like he could be my father's nonexistent brother.

But I'd only ever seen my uncle once before.

Leaving Hound's office yesterday.

I looked at him, and then at Mr. Iharos, and the words "He's not my uncle" were there, poised on the tip of my tongue like a diver on the edge of the high board at the Olympics. The diver flexed. The diver was about to take one step forward. The diver turned around and walked away.

"Uncle," I said, "I hope it's not bad news."

"We'll discuss it on the way out," said my uncle, turning to Mr. Iharos. "And thank you so much for your understanding. I can see that David made the right choice sending his boys to Grammar."

As my uncle and I walked away he whispered, "You done good so far, just keep your trap shut until we get outside."

"Of course I will, Uncle," I said.

I had a newfound respect for Hound's capabilities; it wasn't easy to get a kid out of Grammar during school hours.

His Hummer was parked in a side street.

Looking inconspicuous. Not!

"Nice work," he said to my uncle, who kept walking up the street, to disappear into another car.

I got into the backseat of the Hummer.

Hound was wearing his office clothes: a black fishnet T-shirt that revealed some scary pectoral development, black fingerless gloves like those cyclists wear, and black bands around each tattooed bicep.

"This is Guzman," he said, pointing to the person in the passenger seat. "My techie guy."

Guzman was in his twenties, but he was tiny, with tiny little bones. In one hand was a cup of coffee that had the name of the café it'd come from – Cozzi's – written on it. In the other was his phone: a Styxx, of course, the brand of choice for most tech-heads.

"Hi, how it's going?" I said, extending my hand.

Guzman ignored it, however. Preferring, instead, to fix me with a stare of such malevolence it would have caused the instant demise of any animal smaller than a canary. Or even a canary if it had preexisting condition, like a weak heart.

"You ready to boogie?" said Hound.

"Look, you may have overestimated my abilities," I said.

A snort of derision from Guzman.

"Nonsense!" said Hound. "You found the Zolt, you hacked into Diablo Bay."

He was right: I did find the Zolt, I did hack into Diablo Bay, but that was different, that was The Debt. And this was … actually what was this, apart from some dumb contra deal I'd made?

Hound handed me a manila folder. "Here's our client."

"*Andre Nitmick*," I said, reading the name scrawled on the front.

"Also known as Andrew Nitmick, Andy Mickets, and so on," said Hound.

I opened the folder to reveal a photo of Andre Nitmick. He didn't look much like a criminal. More like the bassist in a heavy metal band. One who liked to eat a lot. Under the photo was a copy of Andre Nitmick's criminal record, or what there was of Andre Nitmick's criminal record. Unsolicited sending of bulk email, identity theft, fraud, and he didn't seem to be a particularly careful driver.

"He's not exactly public enemy number one, is he?" I said.

"Don't be fooled – major player," said Hound de Villiers. "The rat didn't turn up for court, so he owes me a packet."

As he spoke he glared at Guzman as if he had something to do with this.

"I'm just not sure how I can help," I said.

Another snort from Guzman.

I was starting to wonder if he could actually speak in English, or only communicated using snorts of varying modulation.

"We've got a fair idea where the rat is hiding," said Hound. "We just need to flush him out."

Guzman shoved a laptop in my direction.

"Got all the software you'll need on there," he said. "Brutus, RainbowCrack, PacketStorm, John the Ripper, Nmap, NetStumbler, WireShark."

So he could talk. Sort of. I'd never heard of any of these programs and wouldn't have a clue how to use them.

I knew Hound wasn't going to believe me if I said this, though. As far as he was concerned, I was the black-hat hacker from hades.

"I assume it's also got Zatopek on it," I said, giving the name of the champion Czech long distance runner of the forties and fifties.

"Zatopek?" repeated Guzman. "Never heard of it."

"Really," I said, feigning surprise. "You've never heard of Zatopek? Well, I guess it's not the most user-friendly program. It's used by your more elite hacker."

"You can download it, can't you? It must be online somewhere," he said.

"Download Zatopek?" I said as if this is the most ridiculous thing I'd ever heard. "It's on my computer at home. We'll have to go get it."

Guzman mumbled something.

"If the kid needs his hardware, the kid needs his hardware," said Hound, starting the Hummer and pulling out onto the street.

We took the entry ramp onto the freeway and he turned the gangsta rap on the stereo up to a volume that could be most usefully described as "pumping."

As we slalomed through the traffic I realized

something: despite not really having a clue what I was doing, despite not having received the third installment, despite hanging out with the scariest human being I'd ever hung out with, I was actually, sort of, kind of, having fun.

PHISH WEAK

Picking up ClamTop wasn't an issue. I knew that Mom wouldn't be home, that she always spent Wednesdays at the office of her charity, the Angel Foundation.

I got Hound to park outside the Halcyon Grove gates while I went in to get the hardware.

There was a van, *Komang Pool Cleaning* written on its side, parked in the driveway of our house. As I kept walking, the pool guy came into view, scooping the leaves from the pool's glittering surface.

I was used to seeing different pool guys of all shapes, sizes and leaf-scooping ability, but there was something familiar about this one.

As I got closer I could see why. The ponytail. The diminutive runner's physique. The baggier-than-baggy shorts. The pool guy was Seb!

Seb my old running mate. Seb who I'd totally lined up for a scholarship at my school. Seb who hadn't even bothered to turn up for the interview. Seb who I'm pretty sure had set me up at Preacher's Forest. Seb who had been in that white van after the first running of the state titles. Seb who I hadn't heard from for ages, who even seemed to have ditched his old phone number. And here he was, scooping leaves out of my pool.

No, it can't be, I kept telling myself as I got closer.

But it was him, all right.

Seb, I wanted to yell. What are you doing? Get away from my house!

But in the end it was just too weird seeing him like that, too random, so I said nothing, and hurried inside to get ClamTop.

When I came back out, Seb, and the van, had gone.

As I got back into the Hummer Hound said, "So what does a house in there set you back?"

"I'm not sure," I said, and it was the truth because I really didn't know.

"Ball park?" said Hound. "One mil? Two mil?"

"I really don't know," I said. "You'd have to ask my dad."

Hound thought about this for a while and said "Too far from the water for my liking. My place, I got the ocean at the front door and the river at my back step."

"Nice," I said.

As we sped away from Halcyon Grove something occurred to me: would the ClamTop actually work?

I mean, this wasn't strictly The Debt, was it?

Well, if it didn't work it didn't work. It wasn't as if I was going to lose a leg over it.

I'll give Hound one thing: he sure knew his way around the Gold Coast, especially the spaghetti of freeways between the coast and the hinterland. And although the Hummer had sat nav, Hound didn't take any notice of it. In fact he seemed to take pleasure in doing exactly the opposite of what it suggested.

"Take the next turn right," said Sat Nav.

"Not on your nelly," said Hound.

We jumped from one freeway to another and in no time at all we were in Southport. Hound parked opposite the rat's nest, a multistory apartment building with a high wall around it and a security entrance.

"Why don't you just bust in?" I said to him. "Like the cops do on TV."

"Because we're not cops on TV," he replied. "We're private investigators and we don't have those powers. Especially not in this country, this nanny state. We have to work smarter."

"I'm not even armed," he continued, reaching under the seat and pulling out a can of Mace. "This is all I carry."

I thought of all the photos on his office walls – it certainly wasn't cans of Mace he was toting in those.

"And you're sure he's in there?" I said.

"The intel's gold-plated," said Hound, looking over at his tech guy. "Isn't it, Guzman?"

"He's in there," said Guzman.

"All you need to do is lure the rat out so we can nab him," said Hound.

"And he's definitely connected?"

"You saw his rap sheet – do you think this rat could survive without the net?"

Hound was right.

Once my family went on vacation to this tropical island in the Pacific. The brochure said that there was Wi-Fi available but when we arrived there was nothing but sand and water and swaying coconut palms. Miranda said that she'd be okay, but as the days went by she seemed to get smaller, thinner, weaker. In the end we cut the trip short so she could get back online, get herself a lifesaving transfusion of data.

I opened my backpack, removed ClamTop, placed it on my lap.

"What is that?" said Guzman. "I've never seen anything like that before."

"It's a limited edition model," I said.

"PC or Mac?"

"Neither, actually."

"So what operating system does it use?"

"Linux," I said, though I really only had a vague idea what Linux was.

"Oh, Linux," repeated Guzman. "Sweet as."

"Give the kid some room, can ya?" said Hound, lighting up a cigarette.

"You smoke?" I said.

"Only when I'm stressed," he said.

If he was stressed, what was I?

The other times I'd opened ClamTop I'd done it vocally, by saying the word "open."

But there was no way I wanted to go all Ali Baba here, especially not in front of Guzman.

So I closed my eyes, concentrating my thoughts on one word, one request, one command.

When I opened them again ClamTop was still closed. And the thing about ClamTop is that when it's closed it really is closed. Not like a suitcase, or a normal laptop. Even when they're closed it's easy to see that, given the right action – a twist of a key, an unlatching of a latch – they could be opened. The ClamTop, however, looked seamless, hermetically sealed.

"Everything okay?" said Hound, expertly directing a stream of smoke through the small gap in the window.

"Okay," I said as again I screwed my eyes shut.

Concentrating, lasering all my thoughts onto this one word, this one action.

The tiniest of clicks.

I released my eyes and – ohmigod! – the ClamTop was open, its screen flickering to life.

"Wow!" I said as I scanned the list of networks available in this area.

"What's up?" said Hound, ashing his cigarette in the ashtray.

"There sure are a lot of networks around," I said.

"No kidding," said Guzman.

"You'll sort it," said Hound confidently.

I started scrolling down, looking to see if any of them obviously belonged to the rat.

But after several screens I realized how stupid that was.

A career criminal wasn't going to call his network ANDRENET or NITMICKHOME or FindMeAndPut-MeInJailNet.

In fact, a career criminal wasn't even going to use his own money to set up a network. A career criminal, especially a black-hat hacker, was going to steal himself some bandwidth, he was going to piggyback on somebody else's Wi-Fi network.

So I sorted the list into unsecure and secure networks, figuring that as an unsecure network was easier to hack into, that was the one he'd use.

But I soon realized that I was probably wrong about that as well.

For an elite hacker, a secure network didn't present that much of a challenge. Maybe five more minutes of their time.

And then they knew that nobody else – except a fellow elite hacker – could access their computer.

So I switched my focus to the secure networks. Which narrowed it down to around a hundred.

I sorted these according to broadband speed, figuring that Nitmick, like most geeks, also had a pathological need for bandwidth speed.

I cracked open SHIVANET, the network on top of the list.

Hound was engrossed in a book, *The Seven Habits of Highly Effective Private Investigators*, but I could see that Guzman was trying to check out my screen, see what I was up to.

I positioned ClamTop so he couldn't. I didn't want him to see how easy ClamTop made it all.

There were five computers connected to SHIVANET, but it looked like only one was active.

I brought this computer up, its desktop cloned to my screen.

Somebody was playing Second Life.

Yes, maybe Nitmick spent his days playing Second Life, but somehow I doubted it.

I went to MYWIRELESS, the next imaginatively named network on the list. This only had one computer connected. Its owner was on Facebook, telling everybody how they had a cheese and ham sandwich for lunch. With lots of grainy mustard.

Again, I assumed this wasn't Nitmick. Hoped it wasn't Nitmick. That he wasn't this big a loser.

Eleven networks, twenty-five computers and an hour and a half later and I still hadn't found Nitmick.

Hound was still reading his book. And Guzman was doing something on his phone.

I cloned another desktop and as I did I noticed something I hadn't noticed before: on the bottom right-hand corner of the screen a tiny red light, with the letters *REC* below it, was blinking.

I didn't investigate further, however, as I was distracted by the desktop that I'd just cloned.

The wallpaper was an image of champion UFC fighter Brock the Rock, in triumphant pose, muscled arms thrust into the air. The desktop was so cluttered, though, that much of the Rock's six-pack splendor was obscured by opened programs.

The only other person I knew who could cope with as many programs as this open at once was Miranda.

There was something called Crossword Maestro, and along the top of the screen were live CCTV feeds, which I assumed had been ported from the building's security system.

They showed the corridor. The front entrance. The underground parking garage.

A PDF file was open. Under the title "Authorized Component Suppliers" was a list of fifty or so companies and their addresses. The document was watermarked "Styxx Secure Document."

This had to be him, but I needed proof.

I went to Internet Explorer where Hotmail was already open. Suddenly I had a feeling of guilt, almost shame. What right did I have to snoop around in somebody's desktop, somebody's life, like this?

It had been bad enough when I'd done it to Imogen, but at least I knew her. Nitmick was a complete stranger to me.

"You getting anywhere, Youngblood?" said Hound.

I really wished he'd lose the Youngblood thing.

I went to the in-box. The latest message was from eve2412.

My darling Andre ... it started.

Found him!

But I wanted to make really sure before I said anything.

So I went through some of the other email messages.

Apart from eve2412 there were two other senders: SheikSnap@hotmail.com and LoverOfLinux@gmail.com.

I thought it was weird that there were only two, but then I realized that this email address must be a secret one, one that only these select people knew about.

A lot of these emails were in this weird cryptic language. But not all of them, and eventually, after a lot of reading, it became apparent that the three of them were involved in some sort of business venture together. And even though they didn't say they were going to rob a bank or defraud somebody, I still got the sense that this venture was essentially criminal in nature.

The whole thing seemed to depend on Nitmick getting his hacker's hand on a document they called the "Styxx List" from some place they called "the Under World."

I wondered about the PDF I'd already seen on Nitmick's desktop, whether he'd already been successful and this seemingly mundane list of companies was it.

There was also talk of "Cerberus," which I gathered was some sort of radical new technology that Styxx was developing. I couldn't quite work out whether it was a phone, some sort of sensing device, an encryption device, or even a combination of all three.

Whatever it was, it was going to "take market share from all the major players."

I also got the sense that LoverOfLinux and Nitmick didn't have the most harmonious relationship, and that Nitmick had reneged on some promise he'd made.

After the in-box, I went to the out-box and this was where it started to get even weirder.

The emails to eve2412 – and there were a lot of them – were all variations on the same "Pixel, I love you" theme.

But the other emails, the ones to LoverOfLinux and SheikSnap, were written in that cryptic language and didn't really make much sense. Not to me anyway.

Suddenly Nitmick – I assumed it had to be Nitmick – started typing a new message to eve2412.

Pixel, I love you so much my …

"Found him!" I said.

"He's there right now?" asked Hound, putting down his book.

"He sure is."

"Then we need to find a way to flush him out," said Hound.

We sure do! I thought.

Obviously Nitmick loved eve2412 and eve2412 loved Nitmick. And from what I knew, people, even paranoid criminals, will do just about anything for love. They'll even set fire to swimming pools.

I told Hound my theory.

He thought for a while before he said, "Okay, phish the punk."

I'd heard the expression "phish" – who hasn't? – but I didn't have a clue how to do it.

"Phish him?" I said tentatively.

"Yeah," said Hound. "And this is what you're going to do. You're going to send him an email from this Pixel, saying that she's in trouble, that he has to come straightaway."

I remembered all the hacker software on Guzman's laptop.

Surely there was something there that would phish: Microsoft Phish, Adobe Phish, something like that.

And surely Guzman knew how to do it.

"Can't do it from my machine," I said.

"Why not?" said Guzman.

"They'd parse the IP address," I said, repeating something I'd heard Miranda say on the phone once.

Guzman gave me a strange look. "Parse the IP address?"

"Do it, Guzman," said Hound. "The kid's done good."

As Guzman powered up his laptop I could see everything he was doing.

He brought up a program called "Nuclear Phishing."

I read out the email address and he tapped away.

"Bombs away?" he asked, his finger hovering over the enter button.

"Bombs away," said Hound.

Guzman hit enter.

I watched proceedings on my screen.

Nitmick was in the middle of typing one of those typically weird emails to SheikSnap@hotmail.com – *If that's the case, bolt's got the number on "a mundane glove," all mixed-up, next to the tiny Phosphorus Mountains* – when the phished email from eve2412 arrived.

He opened it immediately.

Rapidly typed a reply: *Pixel, what's wrong?* The send button illuminated.

Now we had a problem: what if the real eve2412 was online, what if she replied?

"Quick," I said. "Send another email that says *Come now*."

Guzman did as I asked.

Again I watched as Nitmick opened this email.

As he typed a single-word reply – *Coming* – and sent the email.

"He's on his way," I said.

Nitmick left his computer logged on, so I could see him exit his apartment on the CCTV monitor.

"He's getting into the elevator," I said.

"Too easy," said Hound. "We'll grab him when he hits the street."

I watched as the elevator opened on the ground

floor and Nitmick emerged.

"He's coming through the front exit," I said.

The rat was out of his nest, and the rest was surprisingly easy.

As he wobbled up the street, towards where the Hummer was parked, Hound jumped in front of him. And even though Nitmick was big, he was sit-inside-all-day-and-eat-junk-food big and he was no match for the enormous Hound with his fishnet T-shirt, scary pectorals and can of Mace.

Hound snapped the handcuffs on Nitmick before frog-marching him over to the Hummer. Opening the back door, he shoved him in next to me. Immediately the smell hit me: BO. Sit-inside-all-day-and-eat-junk-food BO. BO that had so much presence I reckoned they'd charge Nitmick for two tickets when he went to the movies.

Hound got back behind the wheel.

"So I gather there's nothing wrong with Pixel," said Nitmick, glaring at Guzman.

"As far as we know, Pixel's fine," said Guzman.

Nitmick seemed about to say something, but Guzman said, "Probably better if you keep your mouth shut now, Andre."

Nitmick kept his mouth shut.

These two know each other, was my immediate thought. *And know each other well*.

"I don't like using dirty tricks like that," said

Hound. "But you really gave us no option, Andre. Why the blazes didn't you turn up at court?"

"Court?" Again Nitmick glared at Guzman.

"That big building with all the lawyers inside it," said Hound. "Your hearing was last week."

"So what happens to him now?" I said.

"Andre's off to the monkey house, I'm afraid," said Hound.

"So he can't get bail again?" I said.

"Maybe, if he asks nicely enough. But Andre's got bigger cash flow problems, haven't you, Andre? And none of his so-called friends are willing to stump up for him. As for his family, what family? They gave up on him years ago."

"So who owned me?" said Nitmick, his eyes moving from Hound to Guzman, before they finally rested on me.

"You?" he said.

I really didn't like his doubting tone.

"Yes, me," I said, and I added, "you're lucky I didn't trash your hard disk while I was there!"

"Steady, cowboy," said Hound. "Our job is to help people build their lives, not destroy them."

Hound started the engine, turned the rap up to volume that could this time usefully be described as "earsplitting" and we headed back towards the city.

As we hit the freeway Hound looked at his watch

and said, "We should be able to get you back to school in time for the last period."

"School?" I said, thinking that was the last place I wanted to be after a hard afternoon's hacking.

"He who opens a school door," said Hound, scary eyes, scary pectorals, "closes a prison."

GOOGLE IS NOT YOUR FRIEND

When I got home, I jumped straight onto my computer.

Brought up Google.

Typed in *Styxx List*.

Hit enter.

I got a few results but they didn't make much sense, not in the context in which I wanted them to make sense, anyway.

I went outside, to the side of the pool, to where I knew Miranda would be doing her tai chi exercises.

"Hi," I said.

"Hi," she replied.

She went into a move I've never seen before: standing on one bended leg, she moved both arms in widening circles.

"Wow, what's that?" I asked.

"It's one I invented," said Miranda. "I was thinking of calling it the Inebriated Emu."

"Catchy," I said.

I waited until she'd finished the Inebriated Emu before I hit her with the real purpose of my conversation. "Have you ever heard of the Styxx List?"

"What is it with you?" she said. "One day it's all about running round and round in a circle, and the next you're suddenly the geekiest kid in the whole of Queensland."

"So you've never heard of the Styxx List?"

Miranda took a small white towel and wiped her face with it.

"Styxx as in s-t-y-x-x?" she said.

"That's right, as in the phones. I typed it into Google and all I got was rubbish and I know for sure it's not rubbish."

Miranda smiled an annoying smile, like I was her dumb little brother or something.

"What?" I said.

"You people," she said. "You all think Google's your friend."

"Google is my friend!" I said.

And as I said this, half jokingly, I realized how true it was: at least Google, unlike Imogen, still talked to me, at least it still answered my questions. And if it wasn't just a search engine I'm sure it would stand at the window in the morning and give me a little Google wave as I started my run.

"Maybe, but it's not going to tell you everything,"

said Miranda.

"So what are you saying, that there definitely is a Styxx List but Google doesn't want me to know about it?"

"That's exactly what I'm saying."

"It censors the results?"

Miranda nodded.

"Why?"

"Obviously, because it wants to protect Styxx."

I must've look doubtful, because Miranda launched into further explanation: "Look, if you're in China and you type in *how to escape from China*, do you think Google's going to tell you exactly which bus to catch and what time it's leaving?"

"They've got Google in China?" I said.

"They've got Google everywhere," said Miranda. "It's just not the same everywhere."

"Anyway, forget Google. Have you personally heard of a Styxx List?"

"Leave it with me," said Miranda, flexing her knees, bringing her palms together.

But then she stopped whatever it was she was doing to say, "He's so hot!"

"Who's hot?" I said, but by the time I'd finished saying that, Seb came into view on the other side of the pool and the question became redundant.

"The pool guy," she answered. "And he's smart, too."

63

"You talked to him?"

"Yes, I talked to him. They are capable of rational discussion, you know, the people we employ."

"Really?" I said.

"I bet you didn't know that Hue Lin has a PhD," she said, referring to our Cambodian cleaner.

"Don't be stupid," I said.

"You should hear yourself, you racist," she said.

"She's got a Masters, not a PhD," I said, before I got the conversation back on track. "What did you and the pool guy talk about?"

"Stuff," said Miranda, raising her eyebrows.

I knew exactly what Miranda was doing: the because-I'm-older-than-you-I've-got-such-a-handle-on-this-stuff thing. And do you know what? She probably did.

So I let her get on with the Arthritic Kangaroo or whatever she called it, and I walked back along the edge of the pool.

As I did I had to admire how clear the water was, how free of leaves. I had to hand it to Seb, he really had it looking great. I walked past the pump room and I heard a noise from inside. Not the usual whirring, pumping sound; this was a sort of electronic beeping.

Strange, I thought.

When we were little kids the pump room was absolutely off limits. You could see why, too – with all its pumps, and electronics, and chemicals, it was a good place for a kid to end up dead. And I remembered thinking that when I grew up, when I was allowed, I would so make up for this, so spend serious time in the pump room. But here I was, sort of grown-up, and I'd been in there maybe twice. So when I opened the door to look inside I didn't immediately think *Wow, that's weird* or *There's something not quite right here.*

There was a whole lot of pipes, and a whole lot of electronics, and a whole lot of chemicals, enough to kill a kid.

But I had this feeling – and that's all it was, a feeling – that there was something different about it.

So I took a closer look, my eyes scanning the room, taking in each feature in turn. Firstly the pumps, and the water heater, and the pipes. They all looked pretty normal to me. Then the big plastic containers in which the pool chemicals were stored. Again, they looked pretty normal. Lastly my eyes stopped on the electronic console.

I guess you had to be a pool guy to really understand what was going on with this, because it was pretty complicated: there were switches, and lights, and meters, and none of them were labeled.

A spaghetti of wires and cables went in and a spaghetti of wires and cables came out. But as I moved closer I noticed something: one of these wires, light blue in color, looked newer than the others.

Although I was no electrician, I could understand what was happening: these wires were supplying electricity to parts of the pump room that needed it. Like arteries carrying oxygen-rich blood to parts of the body.

When I noticed that the light-blue wire ran all the way up the wall and then across the ceiling, I got quite excited. But when it disappeared into a hole, my excitement faded.

Where's it gone now? I wondered.

I went back outside and checked out the roof of the pump room, or what I could see of the roof of the pump room. Because it was flat, not pitched, most of it was hidden from view and I couldn't see anything except a couple of vents.

Time to let go of this, I told myself.

But another part of me wasn't giving up so easily.

Another part of me went all the way to the back shed to get a ladder.

After propping the ladder against the side of the pump room I carefully climbed up it until I had a better view of the roof. But I still couldn't see anything. So I climbed further, all the way to the second-to-last rung. My knees resting on the top rung, I leaned further in.

And there it was.

It was just a small black box, but it looked like it had been recently installed, and I could see the light-blue wire going into it.

And then I thought I heard the scuff of footsteps and the ladder wobbled and I lost my balance and both I and the ladder came tumbling down. As I did I grabbed at the gutter, managing to get both hands on it. So now I was dangling, a drop of about three meters below me.

Only three meters but more than enough, if I fell, to twist an ankle, to break a leg, to demolish any hope I had of going to Rome for the World Youth Games.

My fingers were slipping.

And then, miraculously, there was something solid under my feet.

I looked down.

The ladder.

Holding it up was Seb.

"Okay," he said. "I've got you now, Dom."

I climbed down slowly, testing the weight of each rung.

"That was close," said Seb. "Lucky I came along," he added.

And again, I didn't know what to think. Had he knocked the ladder over in the first place? Or had it just slipped, and he had indeed just happened to come along at the right moment?

But further thought along these lines was curtailed by Mom's voice saying, "Dom, you there?"

And the appearance of Mom herself, dressed up, looking stunning.

The sort of mum other boys looked at. Said things about, like, "Is that seriously, like, your mum?"

"What's happening here?" she said.

There's this strange little black box on the roof. Our pool guy probably just tried to kill me. My life is a mess. A number of answers came to mind, but that's where they stayed.

"I was having a look up there," I said, pointing to the roof.

"What in heaven's name for?"

"A pair of swimming goggles," I said.

Mom threw Seb a half smile and shook her head as if to say, *My second-born has gone bonkers,* then she said, "Your dad and I have got this thing on tonight but I wanted to remind you about shopping on Saturday, okay?"

"Where you going?" I asked, which was pretty weird because I never asked Mom where she was going.

Usually, it was like "whatever" meets "who cares?"

Mom was surprised, too, because she gave me a funny look before she said, "Ron and Justine's."

"Ron as in Ron Gatto?" I said.

"That's right," said Mom.

Again, that image, those four men in suits: Rocco Taverniti, Ron Gatto, Dad, and that other man.

It was like this billboard had been erected in my mind. No matter where I went these days, I seemed to pass it.

Ω   Ω   Ω

Later that night I was watching a movie on cable. Miranda, carrying a bowl of corn chips, sat down in an armchair, tucking her legs up under her.

"What's this?" she said.

"*The Godfather*," I said. "The second one."

"Oh," said Miranda, and I wasn't sure if it was an approving or disapproving "oh."

Because, as far as I knew, all *The Godfather* films were a Johnny-Depp-free zone.

Still, she seemed to quickly get engrossed, chomping her way methodically through the chips.

When the film had finished she said, sort of casually, "Oh, by the way, I did some asking around about that Styxx List thing."

"You did?" I said, trying for a similar casual tone, but failing miserably.

"Apparently it's got something to do with the Cerberus, this top secret new-generation gizmo that Styxx's supposedly been developing."

"Gizmo?"

"That's the weird thing – nobody's really sure if

it's a phone or not. Actually, nobody's really sure if they really are developing it or not. Ever since it came on the market, Styxx has loved playing these sorts of games. Out-Apple-ing Apple, if you know what I mean?"

Actually I didn't have a clue what she meant, but I gave a knowing smile anyway.

"Fascinating stuff, actually," said Miranda. "There's talk it might even be running Linux or another open-source operating system."

I knew from the way she said it that this was a big thing but I wasn't sure why.

"Wow, Linux," I said. "That means…"

Fortunately Miranda jumped in exactly where I wanted her to jump in, finishing my sentence. "That means that it will be incredibly adaptable. Jailbroken without the jailbreak, if you like."

"So it'll be able to run all sort of programs?"

"Just about anything."

Okay, I totally got this: a nerd's dreams come true.

"So if they are developing it, where do they do it?" I asked.

"The Under World, of course."

"Sorry?"

"The Under World. That's what their R&D center is called in the hacker community."

"R&D?"

"Research and development."

"And where is the Under World?"

Miranda shrugged her shoulders.

"You don't know?"

"Not just me – nobody knows. Some people reckon it's out in the desert. Others reckon it's on a ship anchored offshore. It's like the biggest secret there is in computers."

No, it's not, I thought, remembering Nitmick's emails.

Miranda continued. "They don't actually make them there, if that's what you're thinking. Styxx's already famous for getting the parts made in different out-of-the-way places, so nobody really knows what they're for, and then putting all the components together itself."

I thought of the PDF titled "Authorized Component Suppliers" I'd seen on Nitmick's desktop. The one with the Styxx watermark on it.

"So what would happen if somebody got hold of a Cerberus before it was launched?" I said.

Miranda rolled her eyes.

"If you really want to be a nerd, you've got some big-time catching up to do," she said.

"Okay, I'm starting now."

"If they got the Cerberus, every factory in Taiwan would start knocking out Cerberus clones. The market would be flooded with Cerberuses before they were even released."

"So this prototype Cerberus would be worth a lot of money?" I said.

"Little brother, you do have a wonderful grasp of the obvious at times. Yes, it'd be worth a lot of money."

"Millions of dollars?"

"Gazillions of dollars," she said.

Was Nitmick seriously on the verge of cloning a Cerberus? Could a man who had no obvious waistline, who called his girlfriend Pixel, whose BO had its own passport, really be on the verge of making gazillions of dollars? And as I asked myself these questions, I had this strange feeling that I'd had quite a lot lately: that these thoughts weren't private, that somebody else had access to them.

CERBERUS

Mom had been at me for months. "Dom, those jeans are so shabby! Dom, you're growing so quickly!" She'd arranged about a thousand trips, but each time I'd managed to worm my way out of it.

Not this Saturday, though.

This Saturday there was absolutely no way out.

After I finished my regular run, as soon as I walked into the kitchen, she pounced on me. Cat. Mouse. You get the picture.

"We're leaving in half an hour," she said, an uncharacteristic note of anxiety in her voice.

First we were going to some trendy café called Latte Day Saints for breakfast and after that we were going to hit the shops.

"Okay, Mom," I said.

"Half an hour," she repeated.

Mom didn't want to drive herself, so she called a taxi.

What if Luiz Antonio picked us up? I asked myself as we waited. And what if he let on that he knew me? That he'd dropped me off at all sort of dodgy places?

But when the taxi arrived and it wasn't Luiz Antonio driving, I relaxed.

We both got into the backseat, the taxi took off, and Mom put her arm around my shoulder.

I smelled her perfume smell.

"This is nice," she said, and I had to agree, it was nice.

"Tell me about when you acted with Al Pacino," I said.

"Not that old thing," said Mom, her accent already becoming stronger, more Californian. "You don't want to hear that old thing."

"Come on, Mom," I said. "Tell me."

So Mom told the story: how she was a young actress who came to Los Angeles to make it in the big time. How she supported herself by performing at kids' parties. Then her big break: her role in *Charlie's Angels*, "Pretty Angels All in a Row." After that the auditions started coming. One day she was called in to test against the leading man. Mom didn't know who it was going to be but when she walked into the room, it was him, the great Pacino!

"I was so nervous," said Mom, "I thought I was going to puke."

"Can I see the photo?" I asked Mom.

She gave me an aw-shucks-not-the-photo look while she opened her purse and brought it out.

It was only small, like a passport photo, and it was in black and white. I'm not sure how old Mom was in it, maybe still in her teens, but she was really, really beautiful. Movie star beautiful.

She did the scene and afterwards the great Pacino said to my mum, "You've got real presence, babe."

To my mum!

"This do you here, lady?" asked the driver.

"This is fine," said Mom, putting the photo away.

She paid him and she got a receipt because Mom always got a receipt, and we got out and there was a line for Latte Day Saints that snaked around the block.

"Let's just go to McDonald's," I said.

I was getting hungry now and wished I'd gone across to Gus's after my morning run like I usually did for a steaming bowl of ugali.

Mom wasn't going to be put off that easily, though.

"Wait here," she said, and she pushed past the people in the line and disappeared into the crowded confines of the café.

A few minutes later my phone rang. *Mom calling …*

I answered it.

"We're in the corner," said Mom.

"How did you manage that?" I asked her as I sat down at the table.

Mom pointed to the shiny-headed man behind the counter.

"Simon's one of my scholarship boys," she said. "It's his café."

When Simon saw Mom pointing he flashed a smile at us, a smile that wouldn't have been out of place on the Gold Coast Teeth Whitening Center's website. I looked out through the window at the people in the line. They looked back at me. I knew they hated me, and they hated my mum, and I couldn't exactly blame them. But neither did I want to give up my table, to stand in that line for goodness knows how long with a complaining stomach.

The waiter appeared at our table.

"My name is Mylanta," he said, or something like that. "I'm your waitperson and I'll be helping to make your breakfast experience a great success today."

After Mylanta, or something like that, had taken our orders I thought about the work Mom did, how she'd helped all these people through her foundation. I also thought about how it wouldn't be possible if my dad wasn't such a money-making machine.

"Mom, did Dad already have a lot of money when you met him?"

Mom seemed distracted, her eyes darting all over the place, and I had to repeat the question.

Eventually she said, "Your father had gone a long way to laying the foundations for his future success when we first met."

Another question occurred to me, a question I was surprised I didn't know the answer to. But there again, we hadn't had a lot to do with Mom's family. Which made sense, really. She was an only child, and both her parents had died in a plane crash.

"What about when you were growing up? Did your parents have lots of money?"

Again Mom seemed distracted – what was going on with her today?

"Sorry, what did you say?" she said.

I repeated my question.

"Lots of money?" she said, and she had this look on her face as if I'd asked her to travel somewhere that wasn't that nice. Like Brisbane. "No, we didn't have lots of money."

At the next table a family was having breakfast, a couple and their daughter.

The daughter looked about the same age as me, and she was beautiful.

Beautiful in the way Imogen was beautiful, with the eyes and the hair, and the bones in all the right places.

But not beautiful in the way Imogen was beautiful, not wholesome, or vibrant, or fresh.

Maybe she was sick, maybe she even had cancer or something, because she had this haunted look, like death was her bestie.

Or maybe it was something psychological. Like my coimetrophobia. Only nastier.

Whatever it was, I couldn't stop myself from checking her out, from sneaking glances at her.

I noticed that Mom, too, seemed interested in what was going on at the next table.

Again, this wasn't the mum I knew. That mum wasn't a snoop, or a gossip. That mum had too much going on in her own world to bother herself with what other people did.

The girl didn't touch her food, but spent the whole time engrossed in her phone, one of those sexy new Styxx models. Her parents kept trying to include her in the conversation:

"You just loved it in Aspen last time, didn't you, Anna?"

"We had such a lovely time in Paris for your fifteenth birthday last year, didn't we, Anna?"

But when Anna looked up at them, it was with undisguised contempt. And when she looked over at our table and our eyes met, I thought, *Here we go, I'm going to get exactly the same treatment.*

But I didn't.

Instead I got … I'm not sure what I got. Hey, it was only a look. It certainly wasn't contempt. Maybe it was sorrow. Or maybe it was pity. But whatever it was, it sent a jolt right through me.

Could she know? I wondered. Could she possibly know what I was going through?

Mylanta arrived then, plates in both hands, and our eyes disengaged.

But when I was halfway through my eggs Benedict, Anna said in a very loud voice, "I want a new Styxx for my birthday party next Saturday night. I want a Cerberus."

A Cerberus? Had she just said "a Cerberus"? No, that just wasn't possible, it was too freaky.

"A what?" said the mother.

"It's a phone, Mum," answered her daughter.

Her father said, "Sweetheart, we just bought you a new phone."

"Don't sweetheart me, Daddy," she said, her voice getting even louder. "I want the Cerberus."

This time there was no mistaking it – she'd just said "the Cerberus."

Everybody else in the café was looking in their direction, and it was obvious that Anna's parents weren't quite sure what to do.

"We better go," said Anna's mum to Anna's dad, looking around.

"Not until you promise to get me the Cerberus," said Anna, hands clutching the sides of her chair.

"Be reasonable, darling," said Anna's dad. "Where are we going to get one if they don't exist?"

"From him," said Anna, arm outstretched, finger pointing at me. "He has to get me the Cerberus for my party!"

Four days ago I'd never heard of a Cerberus and now it seemed that it was all I was hearing about!

Anna's mum threw me a look – *I'm so sorry* – before she stood up.

"Let's get out of here!" she said to her husband, who was already taking a credit card out of his wallet to pay the bill. When Anna and her parents had left Mom said, "That poor child."

I didn't say anything. I couldn't. There was a shot put in my guts. Was this it: the third installment of The Debt?

This seemed so different from the other two, when the communication had been straightforward. Okay, maybe a talking treadmill wasn't that straightforward, but it was when compared to this.

Then I remembered what Gus had said: that sometimes half the battle was working out exactly what the installment was.

"Dom, are you okay?" said Mom. "Do you know that girl?"

Yes, I told her, *I'm okay*.

No, I told her, *I don't know Anna*.

But if this was it, the next installment, then there were a whole lot of crazy coincidences that didn't make sense.

Like I just happened to be at this café, at this time. Unless …

"Why did you choose this café?" I asked Mom.

She gave me a what-sort-of-question-is-that? look.

"I mean, why didn't we go to Zellini's like we usually do?"

She didn't have to answer, because Simon appeared at our table.

"So glad you could finally make it," he gushed.

There was more gushing, from both Mom and Simon, and I figured now wasn't the time to pursue the matter.

The shopping trip was pretty much a disaster because trying clothes on was the last thing I wanted to do. Mom seemed equally as distracted.

"Dom, I don't think this is working, do you?" she said eventually.

I agreed, it wasn't working.

She extracted some cash from her purse, shoved it in my hand, and said, "Maybe you're better off doing your own thing today."

"Okay," I said, though I think we both knew that the money wouldn't be spent on clothes.

Mom moved in for a hug.

And not a perfunctory before-you-go-to-school type hug either, not even an I-won't-see-you-for-a-week type hug; this was about as serious as a hug can get.

Dom, it said, *I love you, and I'll always love you. No matter what happens.*

Okay, it was a hug, not an email, but take it from me, that was what it said.

S IS FOR STYXX

"An architectural triumph," "a cathedral to technology," "as innovative as the products it sells": people sure got themselves all worked up about the new Styxx Emporium.

Tomorrow's Technology Today, said the sign, in that distinctive Styxx font.

It got me thinking about Styxx, how it had come from nowhere to become a "major player in the smartphone market."

I had to admit, it was a pretty cool place. You entered at street level through a dazzling glass cube, and then descended a glass staircase into the shop itself. It was always crowded, though. Even though it was open twenty-four hours a day, seven days a week, it was always crowded.

I passed a group of excited kids. Apparently the Styxx Emporium now catered for birthdays. Or sPartees as they called them, and these kids were waiting to be shown to their very own sPartee sPace.

I scanned the long line waiting at the counter. Despite the fact that he was wearing too-big clothes and Two Dollar Store bling, I recognized one of the customers straightaway: Bryce Snell. He was this kid who used to go to my primary school. Freckle-Face, we called him, because he had freckles as big as cornflakes. Behind his back, though, because Bryce Snell was a bully. Actually, one of the reasons I first started running was to get away from Freckle-Face Bryce Snell and his Chinese burns. Last time I'd seen him he'd been working at Big Pete's Pizzas but now, apparently, he'd adopted a more urban Afro-American lifestyle.

I walked up to him and said, "Hi, Bryce, long time no see."

Freckle-Face looked me up and down before he said, "The handle's Thuggee Thug, dawg."

"Sorry?"

"My handle, dawg."

"Look, Thuggy Thug, would you consider selling your spot in the line?" I said.

"Thug*gee*," he said.

"Sorry?"

"It's not Thuggy, it's Thug*gee*. You know, with the emphasis on the second syllable."

"Thuggee Thug?"

"You got it, dawg."

"Okay, Thuggee Thug, would you consider selling your spot in the line?" I said.

"How much?" he said.

"This much," I said, holding out some of the cash Mom had given me.

"This some sort of trick, dawg?"

"No trick," I said. "Look if you don't want it, I'll ask the next person."

Thuggee Thug, the freckle-faced gangsta rap artist formerly known as Bryce Snell, took the money and surrendered his place in the line.

"Hey, you can't do that!" came a voice from behind me.

I spun around to see an angry nerd.

Okay, I agree that "nerd," as a term, is pretty useless. There's about a thousand different types of nerd. What was once a species is now a genus.

This nerd was wearing a T-shirt that had one word on it: *gamer*.

I know you shouldn't judge a nerd by its T-shirt, but I was pretty sure that what I had here was a gamer nerd.

"You just can't buy your way in," he said, in his gamer nerd voice.

"Well, I just did," I said.

Although, to tell the truth, I was actually on his side in this debate. But there were other matters to consider, like The Debt.

"It's unethical, man," he said.

I took out my wallet, extracted a twenty-dollar bill, and held it out to him.

He snarled at it, like I'd just offered him a free gym membership.

So I added another one of Mom's twenty-dollar bills to it.

Did he hesitate, was there considerable internal debate as to the morality of my offer? No, his hand reached out and swiped the money. Two minutes later, and I was standing at the counter. My Styxx Knowledge Consultant was one of those people who close their eyes when they talk.

"Hope you didn't have to wait for too long," she said, eyes closed.

There was this kid at school – Ivan Van Berlo – who did this as well and I had the weird thought that perhaps they were related, both carriers of the close-your-eyes-when-you-talk gene.

"Not too long," I said.

"And how may I help you today?" she said, eyes closing.

"I'm interested in the Cerberus," I said.

"The Cerberus?" she said.

"That's right, the Cerberus," I said.

"I think, maybe, you've got some wrong information about our models. Maybe it was the Typhon or the Charon you were after."

"No, I'm pretty sure it's Cerberus."

I was pretty much getting the feeling that I was wasting my time here, as it was obvious she didn't have a clue what I was talking about.

"Okay, thanks anyway," I said when I realized that two security guards were next to me, towering over me.

"Sir, could you please come with us?" one of them said.

"What have I done?" I said.

"Nothing, sir. It's just routine."

I followed them down another glass staircase onto the lower level and into a small room with a white table and a pair of white chairs.

"Please sit down," said one of the security guards. "Somebody will be with you soon."

That soon was almost five minutes, by which time I'd established that I was being monitored, that there was a tiny CCTV camera on the ceiling.

A man and a woman entered the room, both of them wearing black trousers and whiter-than-white shirts.

"Could we see some ID?" asked the man.

"I don't have to show you any ID," I said. "All I did was ask if you had a type of phone."

The woman and the man exchanged looks.

"Who told you about this?" the woman asked.

"I can't remember," I said. "Maybe it was one of my friends who told me about it."

"About what?"

"About the ..." I said, the wheels of my mind spinning hard, trying to come up with a plausible-sounding name.

"About the Pheidippides," I said, remembering the conversation I'd had with Dr. Chakrabarty.

"The Pheidippides?" said the man, and I couldn't blame him for smiling – who would ever call a phone a Pheidippides?

"That's right. My friend told me there was this new model coming out."

"It seems there's been a silly mix-up," said the woman. "How about we give you a voucher for your trouble and forget all about it?"

I left the store with a twenty-dollar voucher (conditions apply) and the knowledge that Cerberus did exist.

Installments on The Debt hadn't exactly been easy so far – turn off all the lights, capture the Zolt – but this one seemed impossible.

Besides, I wasn't even sure it was an installment.

Or was I?

Again, I remembered what Gus had told me about working out exactly what the installment was.

No, this was the installment. It had to be.

As I made my way home it was with the same feeling I'd had before the first two installments: a mixture of excitement and trepidation.

Though in this case there was a lot of the latter. How was I supposed to get something that was only whispered about in the furthest reaches of cyberspace?

NITMICK IN JAIL

Instead of making for my bus stop after school I was going in the opposite way, towards the jail, when Mr. Ryan pulled up next to me in his Prius.

"You heading in my direction today?" he said through the open passenger window.

"I suppose," I said.

"Hop in," he said. "I'll give you a lift."

Teachers at Coast Grammar were definitely not allowed to offer students a lift. But I guess our relationship had moved from the traditional teacher–student model into the area of lawyer–crim.

"So these things are good on fuel?" I said when I got in, which I guess is what 92.6% of people say when they first get into a Prius.

"Just doing my little bit for the planet," said Mr. Ryan, which I guess is how 92.6% of Prius owners respond. "Where you headed?"

I could've come up with a whole lot of places on this side of town – the troll recycle center, Madame Flo's Retirement Home for Overused Emoticons – but I was getting pretty sick of telling lies.

"The jail."

"Oh," said Mr. Ryan, and it was one of those drawn-out "oh"s that teachers specialize in, which are invariably followed by a series of increasingly probing and increasingly uncomfortable questions.

"I wanted to ask about work experience for over vacation," I said, getting in first.

Yes, yet another lie, but what choice did I have?

We were on the highway and Mr. Ryan was concentrating on his driving, on maintaining his miserly fuel consumption.

When the traffic thinned out again, he said, "I've done some more work on that Zolton-Bander thing."

"You have?"

"Yes. There's something not quite right going on here."

He was right – there was something not quite right going on here – but I wondered if he had any idea how not quite right it was.

We arrived at the jail and Mr. Ryan pulled up outside the visitors' reception. I thanked him, got out and watched as the Prius puttered off.

Welcome to the Gold Coast Remand Center, said the sign.

I walked up the stairs, the automatic doors slid open, and I was in the reception area. I took a number 264 ticket from the machine. The electronic board said that they were *Presently serving number 251*, so I had time to have a look around.

Not that there was much to look at, just a shop that sold a few basics like soap and toothpaste and men's magazines.

When my number appeared on the board I approached the window.

"And who are we visiting today?" said the woman.

According to her badge her name was Jandyce and she was wearing the pinkest lipstick I'd ever seen.

"Andre Nitmick," I said.

Jandyce checked her computer screen. "Ah yes, one of our newer guests."

"That's right," I said, getting into the swing of it. "He only checked in a few days ago."

"And if I could see some ID, please?"

I handed her my ID.

"So you're Mr. Borzakovsky?" she asked.

"That's right," I said.

I'd bought the fake ID at lunchtime from Bevan Milne for ten bucks.

"That Russian or something, is it?" she asked.

"Yes, it is," I said, wondering if I should have attempted some sort of Russian accent, like one of the bad guys from a James Bond film.

I also wondered if I should've spent more money and purchased an ID that wasn't so obviously Russian.

Jandyce seemed satisfied with this, though, and banged away at the keyboard.

"Take a seat," she said, handing me a pass. "When they call your name you can go through to the VIF."

"The VIF?"

"Visitor Interchange Facility."

"Oh," I said, before I thanked her.

"It's been my pleasure," she said.

I took a seat and five minutes later there was a voice over the intercom: "Visitor for Andre Nitmick."

First I had to go through one of those scanners, like they have at airports.

"Any metallic objects, keys, belts?" asked the guard, who looked sort of lumpy, like a no-frills sausage on a really hot barbecue.

"No," I replied, but when I walked through the machine beeped loudly, much louder than the ones at the airport, and it felt like everybody's eyes were now on me and my beep.

"Artificial hips, pacemaker?" said the guard.

"Not yet," I replied, quite pleased with my humorous reply, but I could immediately tell from the bored look on his face that about a million witty people had gotten there before me.

"Could you please stand aside while we do a hand scan?" he said.

I remembered then that exactly the same thing had happened to me at the scanner at the power station.

Why had I suddenly become scanner-active?

He passed the hand scanner over me and it made a series of high-pitched robotic noises.

"So no operations of any kind?" he said.

"Just my appendix," I said, resisting the temptation of further humor.

The guard walked over to have a discussion with his less lumpy colleague.

Eventually he returned and said, "You can go on through."

The prison, this part of it anyway, looked like a cheap motel. Not that I'd ever been in a cheap motel, but you know what I mean.

Inmates sat on one side of a table, visitors on the other.

Guards looked on, their faces impassive.

And the whole place smelled like air that had been recycled over and over again, air that had been belched and farted and coughed, re-belched and re-farted and re-coughed, countless times.

It took a while, but Nitmick, in a shapeless brown tracksuit, shuffled in. Poured himself into the seat. Glared at me.

"I wanted to talk to you, Mr. Nitmick," I said.

"And I wanted to talk to you, Mr. Scumbag," he said. "Tell me, did you read all my emails to Pixel?"

"Only the necessary ones."

"You get off on that, did you, you sick piece of scum?" said Nitmick.

This was a bit rich coming from somebody with his criminal record, but I understood how he was feeling: I'd hate it if somebody went through my emails.

"I'm sorry," I said. "I was just doing a job."

"The old 'I was just doing a job,'" said Nitmick. "That's what the Nazis said, you know."

"I thought they spoke German."

"Don't be a dipstick," said Nitmick.

"I want to get you out of jail," I said.

"You put me in jail!" said Nitmick, his voice screeching.

Again, he'd made an excellent point, and I wondered whether he'd been on the debate team at his high school.

"Like I said, I was just doing a job. But now I feel really bad about it, so I want to get you out of here."

"And what do you want from me?"

I lowered my voice. "I want to know about the Under World."

"Do you think I'm an idiot?" he said, standing up and walking off towards the waiting guard.

This was exactly what I'd expected, exactly what I'd envisioned, so why had I hoped it might pan out any differently?

As I walked back through the reception area the voice over the loudspeaker said, "Visitor for Andre Nitmick."

I stopped, watched as a curvy woman in a velvet dress, swathed in scarves, dark eyes ringed with even darker mascara, a crucifix around her neck, made for the door to the VIF.

Ohmigod, I knew her!

I pulled out my wallet, took out a card: *Eve Carides, Numismatist.*

She was the one who had told me that the Double Eagle was a replica, or to use her words, a "fakeroony."

I heard the guard say, "Ms. Eve Carides?"

"Yes, that's me," she replied.

"Mr. Nitmick is waiting for you."

It was her – Pixel!

She disappeared through the door.

The maximum time for a visit was only thirty minutes, so I decided to wait for her. I found a magazine to read. When Pixel reappeared, she was crying mascara-speckled tears.

I stood up and followed her as she made for the exit.

"Excuse me," I said, holding out a handful of tissues.

"Thank you," she said, dabbing ineffectually at her eyes.

When she'd finished she handed me back the now-sodden mass of tissue.

"Look," I said. "I don't know if you remember me, but I came into your shop a few weeks ago."

"The boy with the fakeroony?" she said.

"Yes, that's me," I said. "I'm pretty sure I can get Andre out of here."

I had no idea what to expect. Indifference? Astonishment? Maybe even violence?

But that was not what I got: she took both my hands in hers – they were soft and fleshy – and said, "Hallelujah, let's pray and give thanks to Jesus."

I closed my eyes while she prayed in a voice that seemed all breath. "Thank you, Lord Jesus, for bringing this angel to me today to help guide me in this, my hour of need."

When she'd finished she said, "Okay, shoot. How do we spring my man?"

I shot, telling her how I thought we could spring her man.

When I'd finished she said, "It's a miracle!"

"But remember," I said, "Andre has to tell me what I need to know."

"Don't you worry about that," said Pixel. "Andre does everything I tell him to do."

I went outside and called Hound's number.

He answered straightaway.

"It's me, Youngblood. I'm at the jail," I said. "You said the other day that maybe Nitmick could get bail again."

"I don't want to big-note myself or anything, Youngblood, but if there's one person who could get that tub of lard out from behind bars legally, it'd be me."

"In that case, I'd like you to bail him for me."

"You must be mad," he said. "Why?"

I ignored his question and said, "If you bail him I'll forget about that work you were supposed to do for me."

"What work's that?" he said.

"Remember, my friend Imogen, her father? The deal was that you'd look into his disappearance."

"Oh, of course," said Hound, but it was obvious he'd done absolutely nothing about it. "Anyway, that ain't enough," he added. "Bailing Mr. Nitmick is going to take some doing."

"But you just said that if anybody can do it, it'd be you."

"That doesn't mean it won't take some doing."

"I could do some more work for you," I said. "Guzman's okay, but he sure doesn't have my skill set."

There was a pause at the other end and I knew I had him.

"Okay," he said. "I might even get him out tomorrow morning if I pull a few strings."

"That's great," I said.

"And Youngblood?"

"Yes, Hound?"

"You owe me, now. You owe me big-time."

What's new? I thought. *Is there anybody I don't owe big-time?*

THE
OCTAGON

"And your parents are definitely okay with this?" said Luiz Antonio as I got into the taxi. He was wearing a Silva da Silva cap. A Silva da Silva T-shirt.

"Absolutely," I said, which was only half the truth because Mom wasn't okay with it at all.

She wasn't okay with the UFC.

"It's absolutely disgusting," she said. "The government should ban it."

She wasn't okay with me going to the casino.

"It's just not the place for a fifteen year old," she said.

"I'm pretty sure the venue has a separate entrance," said Dad.

She wasn't okay with me going out on a Tuesday. "It's a school night!"

And she wasn't okay with Luiz Antonio. "Who is this man he's going with?" she said. "This taxi driver?"

But Dad came to my rescue. "It's fine, dear," he said.

"But –" said Mom, but that was as far as she got because Dad, his tone more forceful this time, said, "Dom has to do what he has to do, okay?"

Mom looked at Dad. Dad looked at Mom. There was a whole lot of unspoken stuff going on between them. Eventually Mom said, "Just be careful, okay?"

As we drove along the Gold Coast Highway towards the casino, people were waving to us all over the place.

Wow, I thought. *Everybody's real friendly tonight.*

Then I realized: *Old-school, derr-brain, you're in a taxi!*

The vacant light might have been off, but it was still a taxi, and they were obviously in short supply. We pulled into the casino parking lot, got out, and joined the people making for the entrance. The majority were men, but there were a few women as well, all of whom seemed really well endowed in both the hair and the bosom departments.

Either Dad had gotten it wrong, or Dad had lied, because the venue didn't have a separate entrance to the casino. You went up the same marble steps, through the same doors, but instead of going straight ahead, you turned to the right. Went up some more stairs. I showed our tickets to the usher and he showed us to our seats.

It was such a relief to see Andre Nitmick there, squeezed into his seat, doing the cryptic crossword in the newspaper.

Getting him to agree to this meeting had been so stressful.

"What about at the train station?" I'd asked him over the phone after he'd been bailed. "Like they do in the movies."

"No can do," he'd said.

"We could hire a boat, go out into the middle of the river?"

"No can do," he'd said.

"Robina Mall, then?"

You guessed it: no can do.

"You have to meet with me," I'd said. "It's part of the deal."

"Deal schmeil."

"How do you think Pixel would feel if you went back inside?" I'd said.

Nothing from Nitmick, and I knew I was onto something.

"I think Pixel would be very upset," I'd said.

Finally he said, "Okay, let's meet at the UFC this Tuesday night."

"You're into the UFC?" I'd said, picturing Nitmick with his hundred-plus kilos of finely chiseled flab.

"Of course, who isn't?" he'd said. "Besides, it's

perfect. There's a lot of people. It's noisy. And it's the last place they would expect to find me."

When you talked to Nitmick a lot, which I'd had the misfortune to do lately, then you became accustomed to "they."

"They" were reading all his mail.

"They" were tapping all his phone calls.

I'm sure he thought "they" were also there when he went to the bathroom, monitoring his every movement.

Nitmick was wearing a Brock the Rock T-shirt, and a Brock the Rock cap. I introduced Andre to Luiz Antonio and the two of them immediately launched into a discussion about the relative merits of Brock the Rock and Silva da Silva. A discussion that soon turned very technical. Apparently both fighters were undefeated. While Brock the Rock's strength was his striking with an eighty percent success rate, Silva da Silva was the takedown expert with an incredible eighty-eight percent success rate!

Luiz Antonio and Nitmick kept on talking until two fighters entered the Octagon and the preliminary bout started. And when that finished a new one started up.

By the time the main bout began I hadn't had a chance to say one word to Nitmick. When Brock the Rock and Silva da Silva started laying into each other, the two men jumped up on their feet, screaming their support. But there again, so did most of the people in the stadium. Especially the women with the really big hair/bosoms.

"Rip his head off, Rock!" yelled the one in front of us.

By the third and final round, there was blood everywhere: all over the canvas, all over Brock the Rock, all over Silva da Silva.

Nitmick's face was a violent shade of red, his voice hoarse from the relentless yelling. And Luiz Antonio had reverted to his native Portuguese.

"*Matá-lo!*" he screamed. "*Matá-lo!*"

It was the last few seconds, both fighters were totally exhausted, but they still managed to swing wild punches in the general direction of one another. When the final bell sounded, the two fighters embraced, collapsing into each other's arms, performing a strange staggering dance around the Octagon.

There was tumultuous applause, everybody in the stadium on their feet clapping. Including me.

And then a hush, as the referee announced the winner: "It's a draw!"

The first one in UFC history, apparently. And Nitmick and Luiz Antonio embraced each other, as if they'd been the ones who had just beaten each other to an honorable pulp.

Which was all very amazing. Except that I still hadn't managed to say anything to Nitmick.

"Under World," I whispered to him after he'd released Luiz Antonio.

"Men's," he said.

"Sorry?"

"Bathroom."

I followed him there.

The bathroom was full of men, and the sweat of men, and the smell of men, and men's excited talk: what a great fight it was!

I stood next to Nitmick at the urinal. He unzipped. And though I didn't have the urge, I also unzipped. I mean, it would've been pretty weird not to – there aren't a whole lot of other reasons for standing at a urinal.

"So you like apple pies?" he said.

We could've been in the middle of the river. Or at the mall. Anywhere, really. Talking about the Cerberus. Instead we were in a crowded, stinking bathroom talking about apple, stupid, pies. I hated Nitmick. His paranoia. His insistence that we meet here. But what choice did I have?

"Yes, I like apple pies," I said.

"The new type?" he said. "The type nobody's tasted?"

"That's right," I said.

"They're not available at the shop yet."

"Yes, I know that," I said. "I went to the shop the other day. They even get angry when you ask for one."

Nitmick smiled knowingly at this. "They do, don't they?"

"So if they're not available at the shop, where can I get one?" I said.

Nitmick looked around, swiveling his body as he did so. Not a great idea when you're unzipped.

Eventually, when he was satisfied that there was nobody eavesdropping on our potentially government-destabilizing apple-pie conversation, he said, "You're better off making one yourself."

"I am?"

"Absolutely. Much easier that way. Really, there's only three basic ingredients."

Three basic ingredients?

I thought about it: case, screen, circuit board. He was right, three basic ingredients. And I remembered the emails I'd read between Nitmick and his two co-conspirators, SheikSnap and LoverOfLinux, how I'd had the sense that they each had a task to perform.

"And they're available locally?" I said.

"More or less," he said.

Then I got it: that PDF I'd seen on Nitmick's computer: "Authorized Component Suppliers."

"Okay, can you email me that PDF?" I said. "Sorry, the list of apple-pie suppliers."

Nitmick zipped up, hitched up his trousers.

"Look, kid, I told you I would've done the time no problem. But I was lying. That place was terrifying.

Now that I'm out, I intend to stay out. Pixel and I, we want to get married, have kids. I'm going to get a real job, a Joe Citizen's job. Maybe move into numismatics. No more hacking for me. No more criminal stuff."

"But …" I started, before he cut me off.

"There is no PDF," he said. "I trashed my hard drive."

With that, he washed his hands at the sink, adjusted his glasses in the mirror and walked away from me.

As Luiz Antonio drove out of the parking lot even more people were waving at us. One man actually pulled a handful of cash out of his pocket and shook it in our direction.

"I don't mind if you want to pick up a fare," I said.

Luiz Antonio laughed.

"When I first came to this country, I never refused a fare. Now, though, I know you can't always be working." He pressed a button on the car stereo. It was that song again.

"Bad head and sick feet?" I said.

"*Sim*," said Luiz Antonio. "You have a good memory."

I looked at the faded photo on his license that was affixed to the window. In it he had long hair, a handlebar moustache. He looked like a member of that cheesy band my mum liked, the Eagles.

"So do you have kids?" I asked.

"Three," he said. "And five grandkids."

"Do they live on the Coast?"

"No," he said. "They're back home, in the Cidade Marvilhosa."

The fingers of his right hand tapped a pattern on the dash, before he said, "I came here because the military was in power in my country and it was safer for me to get out. But then I got used to living here, and my family got used to me not living there."

The sick feet song finished and another one started.

"What's this song about?" I asked.

"It's a very sad song," he said.

"What does it mean?"

"Sadness has no end, but happiness does."

I thought of Gus, his leg taken from him. His dead brother. I thought of how Imogen didn't talk to me anymore. I thought of The Debt: how was I ever going to pay this installment?

It was pretty spot on, I thought.

Sadness has no end, but happiness does.

"I want to get out here," I said.

"But ..." started Luiz Antonio, but I didn't let him get any further. I just had to get out of the taxi.

"Please," I said. "Please drop me off right here."

He pulled to the curb.

I got out.

And I started running, not taking any notice of where I was going. Just running, eating footpath.

Away from all that endless sadness.

COZZI'S

I had one of those nights.

Twisting and turning, wrestling with the sheets.

In my head, a procession of images, each more horrendous than the one before. Ending, as usual, with the most horrendous of them all: my leg, freshly amputated, twitching on the ground, while a geyser of blood spouted from my stump.

I woke, cold and sweaty, and stayed like that as the first tentacles of light reached into my bedroom.

When my iPhone alarm went off, the Baha Men once again lamenting the lack of canine-related security, I got up and went for my customary run.

But this morning not even the run had its usual calming effect. The nightmare lingered, twitching stump, geyser of blood.

So from the Coast Home Loans office I pushed it hard, insanely hard.

And when I arrived at Gus's house, red-faced, gasping for breath, he was not happy.

"What in the blazes are you doing?" he said, checking the numbers downloaded from my pulse meter. "Your BPM was sky-high."

"This stuff tastes like crap," I said, pushing the bowl of ugali away.

Actually, it always tasted like crap, but usually it was the crap you ate because it was good for you. Today it was just plain crap.

"I'm going to have a normal breakfast at home," I said, getting up.

Mom was alone in the kitchen and the juicer was juicing. Carrots, beets, celery: you wouldn't believe the stuff she fed it. And always, at the end, a great big knobby knob of ginger.

"You know about the dinner tonight, darling?" she said, sipping the resulting concoction.

"The dinner?"

"Yes, I've told you twice already," she said, a note of irritation in her voice. "There's a few people coming, mostly from inside."

By "inside" she meant from inside the walls of Halcyon Grove.

"And Toby's going to do his ice cream, of course," she added.

"Of course."

"The Jazys are bringing Tristan along," she added. "The doctors want him to start doing normal things."

It just didn't seem fair: if Tristan could start doing normal things, why couldn't I?

"Wouldn't exactly call green tea and lychee ice cream normal," I said, and immediately regretted my words.

"That's not the green-eyed monster rearing its ugly head, is it?"

"Are you asking me if I'm jealous of Toby?" I said, and I was ready for a fight.

I still hadn't quite gotten my head around what had happened on Saturday: had my own mother set up that thing at the café? Was she somehow involved with The Debt?

I could see Mom tense, the knuckles on her hand holding the glass whiten. But then something seemed to come into her face and the knuckles returned to their normal color.

"Let's just all have a nice time," she said, finishing her concoction with a tiny smack of her lips.

"I'm going to get ready for school," I said, making for the stairs.

My phone rang. It was Hound.

"Gotta job for you," he said, his voice full of gravel.

"Good morning to you too."

"Yeah, whatever," he said. "I'll see you at Cozzi's at nine thirty."

"I've got school today."

"Lose it," he said, then he hung up.

Weirdly, I felt relieved. There was no training today so I'd been half thinking of ditching school anyway, and Hound's phone call had sort of legitimized it. I figured that his job probably wouldn't take long, half a day at most, and then I could spend the rest of the day on The Debt.

Grammar was The School That Can't Be Ditched. Grammar was unditchable. Except I'd done it twice already, the first time with ClamTop, the second time without.

I followed the same simple plan as the first time. When Mom dropped me off, I made slowly for the entrance. When her car had disappeared, I pretended that I'd left something behind and headed back to the drop-off zone. From there, I hurried across the road.

This was the most dangerous part of my plan, dodging four lanes of hurtling cars, buses, trucks and various other potentially life-ending vehicles. I made it through, and sprinted on to the park, into some bushes, where I changed out of my school clothes.

I took ClamTop out of my schoolbag.

Open, I thought, wondering whether it would. Again, my ditching school wasn't strictly to do with The Debt.

It opened immediately, however.

Available Wi-Fi Networks, it said at the top of the screen.

I double-tapped on GRAMMARNET.

It was a secure network, it wanted a password.

The password cracker appeared, the little devil doing its devilish dance, the words *cracking password …* underneath.

Again, it took about fifteen seconds for it to start smiling, for the words *password cracked* to appear.

There were hundreds of computers connected to the network. They were arranged alphabetically, however, and it didn't take me long to scroll down and find Mr. Travers's computer, the one he always seemed to be looking at.

When I cloned his desktop, the Computerized Roll Call program was open, and he'd started ticking the names of the students who were present. Albrechtson. *Tick*. Betts. *Tick*.

When he came to my name, he left it blank. I corrected that little omission by moving the cursor to the box next to my name and tapping on the screen. A tick appeared in it. When Mr. Travers had finished, the "send data" button was highlighted. Which meant that an automated text message – *Our records show that your son Dominic Silvagni is not attending school today. Could you please call immediately with an explanation* – would not be sent to both my parents' phones.

I was just about to log off when something caught my eye.

Again, Mr. Travers had his Facebook page open.

He had 524 friends, too. Maybe he wasn't the total loser we all thought he was.

And he'd just made a posting.

Bored, bored, bored. Who thought my life would ever come to this? 30k a year it costs to send a kid to this moron factory. And what do you end up with? Kids who couldn't think their way out of a wet paper bag.

Wow, that's pretty mean, I thought. Followed by, *Wow, that's some good ammo.*

I caught a bus to Surfers. Normally I never sat in the back seat because the back seat belonged to the tough kids, the bad kids. Even though this particular back seat was empty, the tough kids were an invisible presence.

"That's our seat, Grammar boy," they warned me with their silent voices.

Today, however, I sat in the back seat. I'd ditched The School That Can't Be Ditched – again – I was off to meet Hound at Cozzi's; I was as bad, as tough as any of them.

As the bus rollicked along, I thought of all those suckers in class right now, listening to Mr. Arvanitakis going on about photosynthesis. Okay, it was pretty entertaining, because Mr. Arvanitakis had a lisp: photo-thyn-thy-thy, but it was nothing compared to this.

I hit the stop button with my elbow (just like the bad boys).

Jumped off the bus before it'd come to a complete stop (just like a bad boys).

And I thought about dropping a huge loogie on the street (just like the bad boys) but decided against it on the grounds of public hygiene.

Everybody knew Cozzi's; it was one of those places that was always being mentioned in the paper, or on the news. Rarely in the food section, however. More like in the leading-underworld-figure-is-shot-outside-Cozzi's-café section. Or the undercover-police-say-they-have-taped-a-conversation-by-the-accused-at-Cozzi's-café-in-which-the-importation-of-a-large-amount-of-cannabis-was-arranged section.

The café itself was tiny, a hole in the wall, but rickety wooden stools stretched out along the footpath in either direction.

As I walked inside, Guzman passed me going in the opposite direction carrying a to-go coffee. We exchanged pleasantries – he snarled at me, I glared at him – before we continued on our ways.

"Do you do mocha lattes?" I asked the man behind the counter.

He was one of those stubbly men who could probably spend their whole life just shaving. You know, like the Sydney Harbour Bridge – once they're finished painting at one end, they have to start again at the other end.

"Either you order a real coffee or you go

to Starbucks," he said, except he didn't exactly call it Starbucks.

I felt like he'd seen straight through my newly acquired back-seat bad-boy persona to the little rich kid beneath.

"Can I have an espresso, please," I said.

His expression still hadn't changed, so I added, "Make it a triple shot."

He smiled at that, calling out my order to the barista in a language that was not Italian. It sounded like the language Saïd Aouita, Noureddine Morceli and Hicham El Guerrouj spoke.

"So you're not Italian?" I said.

"Where's the law that says only Italians can make good coffee?"

I really wished I could've rewound the last five minutes.

"Do I need a number or anything?" I asked.

"Just take a seat, Snake'll find you."

I went outside, found an empty stool and waited.

Two kids, a boy and a girl, both around my age, sat down at the table behind me.

The first one I knew: it was Brandon.

But this Brandon was thinner than the Brandon who I'd seen at the hospital, at the cinema, and at the arcade.

"Needle and the Damage Done," I told myself, thinking of the Neil Young song Mr. McFarlane had used in one of his English classes.

His companion was the girl who'd been with him on the first two occasions: short dark messy hair, pale skin, big eyes; she looked a bit like an anime character.

They looked at me. I looked at them.

But then Snake – tight jeans, sharp boots, retro fanny pack – found me, just as the man said he would, and I turned my attention to the coffee he handed me.

"That'll kick-start your day, amigo," he said, taking out his phone from the fanny pack, swiping pages like crazy.

"That the new Styxx Charon?" I said.

"Totally kicks butt," said Snake. "Can't keep my hands off it."

"Order, Snake," boomed a voice from inside the café and Snake shoved his phone into his fanny pack and took off.

Jobs, I thought, *they sure do get in the way.*

The first sip of my triple-shot espresso and a bomb exploded in my mouth. It was hot and it was bitter, and the caffeine rush almost knocked me off my tiny wooden stool. I managed to register that Hound had arrived, his black Hummer pulling up in a No Parking zone. He got out and there was a lot of denim: denim jeans and a denim shirt and a denim jacket.

In my world, in my school, even double denim

was a serious crime; you got sentenced to a dead leg for that, or your underpants full of slushie. But this was triple denim – triple denim! – and nobody seemed to care.

Everybody, it appeared, knew Hound. There was a lot of blokey interaction – complicated four-part handshakes, rib-cracking backslaps – before Hound eventually got to me.

"Drinking the real stuff," he said, indicating the cup.

"Real coffee," I said. "You want me to get you one? Kick-start your day, amigo?"

"Can't stand the stuff," said Hound. "No good for the nerves."

Snake appeared with a cup of tea on a saucer and handed it to Hound. Hound sat down on a stool and took a delicate sip.

Two large men in large suits approached.

"Hound, we need to talk," said the taller of the two.

"This is my associate, Dom," said Hound, standing up.

I stood up to shake each man's hand and sat down again.

They started talking to Hound, but although they spoke in English, I didn't really understand a lot of what they were saying.

"Coast Home Loans" I got. How could I not? They

seemed to have an office on every corner. But when they started talking about an associate of theirs who was "well out of his depth" and was being "leaned on" I got totally lost.

Hound said that he'd do some digging.

The three men shook hands and there was a flash.

I looked around to see a man standing half on the road and half on the footpath, with a camera pointed towards us.

Another flash.

The photographer ran across the road and got into a waiting car.

"What was that?"

"Papers," said Hound. "For the social pages," he added, with a smile.

"Do you think I'm in it?" I said, thinking that it wouldn't be such a good look for somebody ditching school.

"Maybe," said Hound. "But don't worry, they'll Photoshop you out."

When the two men had gone we sat down again and Hound pointed to my coffee. "You want another one of those?"

"No, I'm good," I said, my nerves jangling like the school caretaker's keys.

"Okay, let's get down to business."

"Let's."

"It's Guzman," he said. "I reckon he's dudding me."

"Dudding you?"

"I'm not sure how, but I've just got this hunch."

"So what do you want me to do?"

Hound took out a piece of paper and a pen and wrote three phone numbers down. "These are his numbers," he said. "But from what I understand, he mostly uses the last one."

Then he wrote an address under that.

"And this is where the maggot lives."

He handed me the paper and stood up.

"I want you to find out what he's up to, Youngblood."

As I watched him get back into his ridiculous Hummer I really wished I'd said something. Something like: "This wasn't part of the deal." Or, "I'm not going to do this." Or, "Even tough guys like you can't get away with triple denim." Okay, forget the last one. But I'd already decided that I wasn't about to start snooping on Guzman. I didn't like him much and he probably was dudding Hound, whatever that meant, but that was none of my business. Besides, there were debts and there was The Debt. If I didn't snoop on Guzman, Hound might turn me in to the cops, he might even beat me up so badly that he'd smash all my teeth and I'd have to survive on protein shakes for the rest of my life, but he wasn't about to take my leg away from me.

It was time to concentrate on getting that Cerberus.

I went to pick up my bag and it was gone. So too had Brandon and his girlfriend. I rushed into the café.

"Somebody took my bag!" I said to the man. "And I'm pretty sure I know who they were."

"Well, you probably should've taken better care of it," he said.

I thought about calling the police, but decided that was probably not the best idea for somebody who was currently ditching the unditchable school.

I called Hound instead, describing Brandon and the girl to him.

"I'll make some calls," he said.

Ten minutes later I received a text from Hound: *sit tight*. Sure enough, five minutes after this, I saw them coming down the street, Brandon with my bag slung over his shoulder.

"That's mine!" I said, moving towards him.

Brandon coughed, a hacking cough that seemed to make his whole body shake.

"It's okay," said the girl, putting her hand out to stop me. "We're here to give it back to you."

There was nothing anime about her voice – it had a sort of toughness about it, a voice you'd think twice about messing with.

"It's okay, PJ," said Brandon. "I can handle this, eh?"

PJ, I thought. I wondered if they were boyfriend and girlfriend. Brandon and PJ, it had a pathetic sort of ring to it.

Brandon coughed again, this one less shuddery than the last, before he put my bag down at my feet and said, "Didn't know you was connected."

Neither did I.

"What is that thing, anyway?" he said.

"What thing?"

"Looks like some sort of computer, eh?"

"Oh, that thing. It's a, um, prototype," I said.

Brandon stood there looking at me with his deep-set eyes, scratching at a scab on his elbow.

"What?" I eventually said.

"Thought you might have something for our trouble."

"You just stole my bag!"

"But we brung it back, didn't we?"

"Come on, Brandon," said PJ. "Leave him alone."

Good idea, I thought, looking at PJ.

She had a sort of half smile on her lips, as if she found it all a bit amusing.

And I guess she had a point. Expecting money for returning a bag you'd stolen – as Peter Eisinger would say, Brandon had some chutzpah.

I took some coins from my pocket – there was

about five bucks – and handed them to Brandon.

Okay, I would have preferred to hand them to her, but it was Brandon who'd asked.

"Wow, last of the big spenders," said Brandon.

As for PJ, she gave me a wink.

Which was pretty weird because nobody, and I mean nobody, under the age of about a hundred and five, winks.

And I almost winked back, but I didn't.

As I watched them moving away, two kids living on the street, I couldn't help thinking about all that stuff we'd learned about in science: Darwin, evolution, survival of the fittest.

How long had they survived on the streets? From what Mom had said, at least a year. Okay, Brandon wasn't looking too hot, but there was something about PJ.

It seemed to me right then that if I was to repay The Debt I'd have to find a bit of what she had, a bit of the street.

I opened the bag, took out ClamTop, made sure it wasn't damaged or anything. As I did, something occurred to me.

I didn't believe Nitmick when he said he'd trashed his hard disk. But as far as I was concerned he may as well have, because there was no way I would be able to get my hands on that PDF.

Once hacked, twice shy – he would be hyper-vigilant now, so vigilant that not even ClamTop would find a way through.

But then I remembered something: the little flashing REC icon.

I put ClamTop on a stool in front of me.

Thought it open.

Previous sessions, I asked myself. Where would it store those? How could I access them?

Almost immediately the words *Previous Sessions* appeared at the top of the screen, and under that a table that detailed the times in the past I'd used the ClamTop, all the way back to the very first time, when I'd cloned Imogen's desktop.

But the one that interested me was last Wednesday.

I touched that part of the screen with my finger. It highlighted – a good sign. I double-tapped on it; a screen popped up.

It looked like a media player, with play, stop, pause and rewind buttons.

I touched the play button.

The list of networks for Nitmick's apartment building appeared.

Nitmick's desktop reappeared.

The PDF titled "Authorized Component Suppliers" with the Styxx watermark.

I hit pause.

Took out pen and paper and copied the list down.

After that I went to the email Nitmick had been about to send to SheikSnap before we phished the crap out of him.

I wrote it down.

If that's the case, bolt's got the number on "a mundane glove," all mixed up, next to the tiny Phosphorus Mountains.

Was this some sort of code or concealment?

I tried a few things: the first letter of each word, the second letter of each word, but I got nothing. It reminded me of something, though.

If that's the case, bolt's got the number on "a mundane glove," all mixed up, next to the tiny Phosphorus Mountains.

Of course! – the clues in a cryptic crossword. Really, I only knew two people who did cryptic crosswords. Nitmick was one, but I couldn't ask him. Not now that he was on the straight and narrow. And the second person?

Why not, I thought, as I closed ClamTop and put it back in my bag. *What have I got to lose?*

CRYPTIC

I waited until school had finished before I changed back into my school uniform and ventured through the gates. Safer that way, I reasoned. There'd be fewer teachers around. But as I hurried towards Hogwarts an authoritative voice said, "Silvagni!"

Shiitake mushrooms! I thought.

But "Shiitake mushrooms!" I didn't say, opting instead for the more conventional, "Yes, sir?"

"I didn't see you around today," said Mr. Travers.

"That's right," I said.

"In fact, I marked you as absent during this morning's roll call."

"That's right, absent," I said.

"So it was with some surprise that a subsequent check of the roll gave you as present."

"That would be surprising," I said. *Especially for somebody who couldn't think their way out of a wet paper bag.*

"Absent but present; now that's an interesting philosophical proposition," said Mr. Travers.

Mr. Travers was enjoying this, the same way a cat enjoys playing with a mouse before he gobbles it up. But what Mr. Travers didn't realize was that this particular mouse had some major squeak-power in him.

"So what are you going to do?" I said.

"Well, I'm afraid I have no choice but to report this to the principal."

"I wouldn't do that if I were you," I said.

"Excuse me?" said Mr. Travers, a how-dare-you-talk-to-me-like-that tone to his voice.

"Because I don't think Mr. Cranbrook would like to hear his school referred to as a 'moron factory,'" I said.

Mr. Travers glared at me, then the cat released his mouse. As he slunk off, I mentally added him to my ever-growing list of enemies. Maybe Mr. Travers wasn't as formidable as some of the others, as Fiends of the Earth, or Cameron Jamison, or the Queensland Police Force, but he was still one more person I had to watch out for in the future.

"Come in!" said Dr. Chakrabarty after I'd knocked on the door to his office.

I went in. There was tinny music playing – Lady Gaga – and I wondered whether Dr. Chakrabarty could possibly be a fan. But then I realized that it was coming from his phone, that it was on speaker and he was on hold.

"Useless Virgin!" he said. "I've been waiting for twenty minutes now!"

"The upgrade?" I said.

"Yes, the upgrade."

"I can come back later," I said.

"No, no, sit down, Pheidippides," said Dr. Chakrabarty. "We can talk while the Virgin decides what she wants to do."

Dr. Chakrabarty, it seemed, had an inexhaustible supply of virgin jokes.

It was the first time I'd been in his office, so after I sat down I took the opportunity to check it out. I'd thought it would be, well, Hogwartian. Piles and piles of dusty books. And other stuff like old statues, old vases, and maybe even some old human remains, bones or something.

But it was very, very Spartan.

Yes, there were some books, but not that many. And they were neatly ordered on the single bookshelf. There was a set of dumbbells sitting in one corner. They were shiny, as if they were frequently used. And on the wall there were three framed photos. The first one was of a building, the Taj Mahal. And the second one was of a person, Mahatma Gandhi. And the third one was of the earth, a globe of brilliant blue and green, taken from outer space.

"You're Indian," I blurted, and immediately felt embarrassed because it sounded sort of racist.

"I was born in that country," said Dr. Chakrabarty. "And now you're wondering what on earth an Indian is doing in Australia teaching the classics."

He was right, it was pretty much what I was wondering.

"It's quite a story," he said. "But maybe not something we should go into right now."

"You, my friend, have progressed in the line and we'll be talking to you real soon," said the young voice on the speakerphone.

"The Virgin," said Dr. Chakrabarty, managing to raise his considerable eyebrows. "Now what can I do for you?"

"You do cryptic crosswords, don't you, sir?" I said.

"Indeed I do," he said. "Or should that be 'Did one die scrambled'?"

Okay, so now he was talking complete nonsense.

"So do you think you could help me with this clue?"

"I could try," he said.

I took out the piece of paper with the clue written on it and placed it on the desk so he could see it.

"I think I know what *if that's the case* means," I said. "And I reckon the rest is some sort of address."

Dr. Chakrabarty studied it for a while, his head cocked slightly to one side.

Eventually he said, *"Next to the tiny Phosphorus Mountains* is interesting."

"I googled Phosphorus Mountains," I said. "It doesn't exist."

Dr. Chakrabarty smiled.

"You're being far too literal, Mr. Silvagni. That's not the way cryptics work. Do you know your periodic table?"

"Yes," I said.

"What's next to phosphorus?" he asked.

I meant I knew what the periodic table was, not what was on it.

"I'll google it," I said, going to take out my iPhone.

"Silicon and sulfur," said Dr. Chakrabarty, before I'd even gotten it out of my pocket. "And what's next to a mountain?"

"A valley?"

Dr. Chakrabarty smiled at me in a way that was sort of half encouraging and half patronizing.

"So if we put them together?" he said, bring his two fists together.

His question hung there, in the space between us. Which was pretty convenient because I needed to look at it for quite a while before I could come up with an answer.

"Silicon Valley?" I said.

"And let's not forget the 'tiny.'"

"Tiny Silicon Valley?" I said. "Where in the blazes is that?"

"Too literal, Mr. Silvagni."

I could see what Dr. Chakrabarty was doing: getting me to exercise my brain rather than just feeding me the answer.

But I hadn't come here to be taught, I'd come here, chicken-like, to be fed.

"Can't you just ..." I started, but then I could feel it, a flurry of caffeine-induced brain activity, and smack-bang in the middle of my thoughts was the answer: "Little Silicon Valley!"

It's what the area south of Brisbane and north of the Gold Coast, where quite a few technological companies had set up, is nicknamed.

"Splendid work," said Dr. Chakrabarty. "Now let's have a look at the rest of it."

He took a pen and underlined *all mixed up* and said, "That's classic cryptic talk for an anagram."

He took another piece of paper and wrote the letters that formed *a mundane glove* in neat block letters in a neat circle.

"Let's see if we can find an address in here," he said. "Well, I can't see a 'street.'"

"No 'road,'" I said.

"Or 'drive.'"

"There's 'avenue,'" I said.

"Is there really?" he said, crossing out the letters *A V, E, N, U,* and *E.* "So there is!"

I felt a flush of scholarly pride, not something that happened to me very often within the hallowed walls of Coast Grammar.

"Now let's see what we can make of these letters we have left," said Dr. Chakrabarty.

"'Mad long'?" I said.

"Nice," said Dr. Chakrabarty. "Mad Long Avenue."

"How about 'Goldman'?" he said. "Goldman Avenue?"

"We could look it up on Google Maps, see if it exists," I said.

"We could," he said. "But let's see if we can work it all out before we resort to Professor Google."

"Okay," I said.

"*Bolt's got the number,*" he read. "Now that's tricky, what number has bolt got?"

Immediately there was a number in my head.

It can't be that, I thought. *It's too random. It's too me.* But Usain Bolt had been all over the news lately because he'd false started at the world championships and as a result had been disqualified.

But Dr. Chakrabarty was still wearing that encouraging smile, so I blurted it out. "Nine point seven two."

"Where did you get that from?"

"Usain Bolt – it's his world record for the 100 meters."

Actually, it wasn't: his world record was 9.58, but

I didn't want Dr. Chakrabarty, or anybody else for that manner, to know the exact address.

Dr. Chakrabarty smiled at me and said, "Great work!"

"That's it?" I said.

"Why not?" he said, writing *972 Goldman Avenue* on the piece of paper and handing it to me.

I thanked Dr. Chakrabarty, and when I was outside I took the pen and changed the *972* to *958*.

THE TWO WARNIES

A taxi passed and I put out my arm.

It stopped and I slid into the back.

"Halcyon Grove," I told the driver.

I slumped back and closed my eyes, half listening to the radio.

A woman was talking: "*It has some of the most spectacular diving sites on the whole east coast and it's an absolute disgrace that this nuclear facility was built there in the first place.*"

I realized that she was talking about Diablo Bay.

"*This bill is going to be debated in Parliament this coming week – what do you think the outcome will be?*"

"*Well, the campaign to close down this facility has such momentum now, I think the Government has no choice but to listen to what its constituents are saying.*"

135

"*The phones are open now and we'd like to hear what you think about this hot topic,*" said the presenter.

I opened my eyes, and noticed where we were.

"Hey, I said Halcyon Grove," I told the driver.

There was no reply.

"Driver, can you hear me?"

There was a *clunk*, and a Perspex shield appeared between me and the front seat. And then a *click* as the doors on either side of me locked.

I bashed my fists against the Perspex, I bashed my fists against the windows, but it was no good; I was trapped.

And the taxi was now barreling down the freeway, heading south.

I relaxed – what else could I do? – and thought about who it was that could be kidnapping me.

The Debt? No, that didn't make sense. Fiends of the Earth? No, this was too slick, too professional for them. Hound de Villiers? Why would he kidnap me? I was already working for him.

When we took the Coolangatta exit, I switched back into alert mode – I needed to remember our route.

We followed this road for eighteen minutes and thirty-five seconds before we took another turnoff, this one signposted as McCallum's Bluff.

I smiled to myself – maybe they weren't as

professional, as slick, as I'd first thought. I'd seen enough movies to know that in situations like this it was almost mandatory for the captor to blindfold the captured.

Then there was a hiss and the back of the taxi filled with a cloudy white gas and I blacked out.

Ω   Ω   Ω

When I came to, my arms and legs were strapped to a wooden chair in a bare room: bare off-white walls, bare wooden floor, no door, no windows, and a double fluoro on the ceiling that threw a harsh light over everything.

The door opened and two men walked in.

They were both wearing Shane Warne masks. Shane Warne, the cricketer.

Which normally would be pretty funny, but right there, right then, the two smiling Warnies scared the crap out of me.

The Warnies stood in front of me.

"You prefer Dom or Dominic?" the shorter Warnie asked.

His accent wasn't Warnie at all, more American.

"I really don't mind," I said. "Are you going to torture me or something?"

"Torture is un-Australian," said the taller Warnie, in an accent that was definitely Australian and sort of familiar.

"We'd like you to tell us everything you know about Yamashita's Gold."

And that's exactly what I did: I told them everything, and I mean everything, I knew about Yamashita's Gold.

When I'd finished, the shorter Warnie said, "Do you know where Otto Zolton-Bander is?"

"Wouldn't have the foggiest," I said.

Shorter Warnie nodded at taller Warnie and suddenly there was an electric shock around my groin area.

"You said you wouldn't use torture!"

"No, what I said was 'Torture is un-Australian.'"

"Let's try again," said shorter Warnie. "Where is Otto Zolton-Bander?"

Even though my groin was still tingling a bit, it hadn't actually hurt that much, but in some ways this was worse, because all I could think was how much it would hurt when it actually started hurting.

I so wanted to tell the two Warnies where he was, and I was even tempted to come up with somewhere, anywhere, but in the end I said, "I don't know, I really don't know."

I readied myself for another shock, but it didn't come.

Instead the taller Warnie brought out the piece of paper that had been in my pocket, the one with the address in Silicon Valley.

"Is this where he is?" he asked.

"No," I said, and started telling the Warnies exactly what it was, but they quickly lost interest.

"Okay, Dom," said the shorter Warnie. "You can shut your gob now."

They left the room for about five minutes.

But then the shorter Warnie returned, holding a black Abu Ghraib style bag.

One part of me said he was going to blindfold me because he was going to let me go. But another part said he was going to blindfold me because he was going to shoot me.

As shorter Warnie went to put the bag over my head, I tried to remain calm. But it was no good, the they're-going-to-shoot-me part of my brain took over and tried to stop him.

"You're not making it very easy for yourself," he said.

"I know," I said, as I tried in vain to bite his hand.

"If you don't stop this, I'm going to have to knock you out again," he said.

I didn't want to be knocked out again, so I forced myself to calm down. Even when the bag slipped over my face, even when the world went Abu Ghraib black. Shorter Warnie then unstrapped me and guided me out of the room and into a car.

"Of course you know it's for everybody's benefit if you keep quiet about all this," he said.

"Of course," I said, realizing then that he wasn't

going to shoot me, because dead men don't talk, dead boys either.

And then I got it, then I knew I'd heard his voice before: it was Cameron Jamison! And I almost said something, but I bit my tongue.

The car trip was about half an hour, forty minutes at the most. And in the beginning I was on high alert, listening for telltale signs that might indicate where I was. You know, the distinctive call of the greater warbler, a bird only found in one particular area of the Gold Coast hinterland, that sort of Sherlock Holmes stuff.

But I soon got tired of that, and just slumped in my seat and tried to relax.

Then the car stopped, the door opened and a gruff voice said, "This is where you get out."

I got out and the car took off with a roar of its exhaust.

I ripped off the Abu Ghraib bag. I was standing at the back of what I immediately recognized as Robina Mall, and three ratty-looking kids were staring at me.

One of them was holding a huge party-size bag of gummy snakes.

"Why've you got that fing on your head?" said one of them.

"I've just been kidnapped and tortured," I said.

"Oh," they said.

I checked my pockets: my iPhone and wallet were still there.

I was just about to get going when I had a sudden, intense craving. "Can I have some snakes?" I asked the kid holding the bag.

"Sure," he said, digging into the bag, holding the snakes out to me.

I took them, crammed them all into my mouth at once and made my way to the bus stop.

By the time my bus arrived the snakes had been ingested, but my mouth was still full of sickly saliva. And my tongue was busy searching for snake fragments lodged in my teeth.

Later, from my position in the back seat, I thought about what had just happened to me. I'd been kidnapped, I'd received a very mild electric shock to the groin, and then I'd been released.

Just a small bump in an otherwise smooth afternoon.

The bus stopped and a mother with two small kids, one on either hip, got on. She put the kids on a seat, but when she got off the bus to get her stroller, they started crying. Nobody went to help her, so I got up, jogged down the aisle and picked up the stroller for her. She thanked me, and I went back to my tough-kid's pose in the back seat.

But when I sat down again, I realized that I had it wrong. It hadn't been just a small bump in an otherwise smooth afternoon.

I'd been kidnapped, I'd been tortured, I'd had a black bag put over my head, and I needed to give this the attention it deserved. A full freaking inquiry. Abu Ghraib style.

It seemed that quite a few people knew I'd been involved with the Zolt.

Some of these people believed that the Zolt knew where Yamashita's Treasure was. Yamashita's Treasure was worth millions. Therefore, if you looked at it from their POV, it wasn't that unreasonable to think that I might also know something about Yamashita's Treasure.

That it would be worthwhile putting on a Warnie mask.

Kidnapping a fifteen-year-old kid.

Resorting to un-Australian activities such as torture.

But why didn't they go the full Abu Ghraib? Why hadn't my knurries been turned into potato chips? Maybe they, the Warnies, just didn't have a taste for torture. All tingle, no shock.

Or maybe they had a better way of getting this information.

I took out my iPhone and ran the anti-spyware app that Miranda had written.

Bingo!

My phone was so infected, it now had something

called Spyware Killer on it. Spyware Killer, apparently, was anything but. According to Miranda's app, it was *highly intrusive* and *very powerful*.

Did I want to *remove this spyware*? the app inquired. I thought about this for a while before I tapped on *Yes*. I already had enough people keeping tabs on me as it was.

By the time I'd finished doing all that I'd missed my stop and had to walk an extra kilometer back home.

LYCHEE

Maybe it was the gas they'd used to knock me out. Maybe it was the tickle to the groin. Maybe it was all those snakes I'd gobbled up. But whatever it was, I wasn't feeling too good: my guts were gurgling and my feet were dragging as I made my way home.

Though my phone kept ringing, jumping about in my pocket, I couldn't even be bothered answering it. Hot bath and then hit the sack, I kept promising myself. Hot bath and then hit the sack.

It was only when I heard a string quartet playing that stuff that string quartets play that I remembered that Mom was having people around tonight.

If this wasn't annoying enough, there was also the fact that Mom never listened to that sort of music; basically she liked the Beach Boys and the Eagles and stuff like that. But just because she was having people around she had to go all string-quartety.

The guests were all arranged around the pool. Waiters swanned about with champagne and hors d'oeuvres.

Just a few people around to watch the semifinal of *Junior Ready! Set! Cook!* and then a bite to eat, Mom had said.

Call this a few people?

Call this a bite to eat?

A girl was floating towards me in a shimmery dress, high heels, hair up.

Who is this? I asked myself, before I realized exactly who it was: my nerdy sister who never, ever got dressed up.

Why? I asked myself.

The answer was three steps behind her. The answer was also dressed up in white shirt and white pants. The answer was our pool guy.

"You know Seb?" said Miranda, and there was no mistaking the pride in her voice.

Seb may have been the pool guy, he may have been kind of short, but he was hot hot hot.

"Seb, you know my little brother Dom?" she said, tousling my hair. Seb sure was doing weird things to my big sister: she was so not the tousling type.

"Where have you been?" Miranda said to me. "Mom's been calling you like mad."

Now Mom was accelerating towards us, facial expression and body language telling me that I was in trouble yet again.

"Some kids tried to rob me," I said to Miranda.

"Some kids tried to rob you?" said Miranda, conveniently, just as Mom arrived.

"Darling," she said, anger becoming concern. "Are you hurt?"

"I'm okay," I said.

"You poor thing," she said.

As we walked back up to the pool I told them what had happened. How I was walking along the street and this gang of kids, including that Brandon who Mom had tried to help once, accosted me. How I managed to fight them off. Okay, it didn't really make a whole lot of sense, but Mom and Miranda seemed to buy it.

"Yeah, I've heard of that sort of stuff happening a lot lately," said Seb.

It was only when Mom and I entered the house together that I questioned just how easily Mom had bought it. I mean, if it was my kid, wouldn't I call the cops or something?

"Do you know who that boy with Miranda is?" I said. "He's actually our pool guy."

Mom looked at me, brow furrowed, shook her head, and said, "That's a very disappointing judgment, Dom."

And it probably wasn't the smartest thing I've ever done when I then said, "Mom, do I really have to come tonight?"

Hot bath, hit the sack – that was all I wanted to do.

Mom opted for a nonverbal reply, fixing me with a look so withering it would've deforested most of the Amazon Basin.

"Okay, I just need to freshen up," I said, borrowing one of her expressions.

I went upstairs.

Firstly I had a shower, trying to convince myself as I did that it was pretty much like a bath except it was vertical instead of horizontal, and a bit less wet. And I have to admit, as I got dressed I did feel better.

My phone beeped.

A message from Hound. *Call me!*

So I called him.

"How'd you do with Guzman, Youngblood?" he said.

"I'm all over it," I said.

"Good," he said. "Because he's acting real suspicious-like."

"Okay."

"And Nitmick dropped in; he was very whiny."

What's new? I thought. Very Whiny was Nitmick's default setting. Except, perhaps, when Brock the Rock was knocking the crap out of somebody.

Hound continued. "He reckons we hacked into his computer."

"We did hack into his computer!"

"No, after that. Later, after I was stupid enough to bail the tub of lard."

"Well, it wasn't me," I said, thinking that whoever had managed to hack into paranoid Nitmick's paranoid computer must really have known what they were doing. "Sorry, but I've got to go."

"Guzman, okay? I need to know what he's up to."

When I eventually got back downstairs *Junior Ready! Set! Cook!* had already started.

It was time to introduce the contestants, and the camera panned from one face to the next.

When it came to Toby's face, we all cheered and yelled.

"Let's everybody keep their fingers crossed for Toby," Mom gushed, looking proudly at her youngest son sitting next to her.

The show had been taped a few days before and even though Toby had been sworn to secrecy I'm pretty sure he wasn't going to sit there, looking so pleased with himself, if he hadn't made the final.

And I was pretty sure Mom wouldn't have invited all these people around for a bite to eat if he hadn't made the final, either.

Sworn to secrecy, my rectal passage.

Eventually the judges announced the finalists

and – what a surprise – Toby was among them. More clapping. More cheering.

Again, I looked over at Toby, expecting more smugness. But that wasn't what I saw, at all. Instead he had this look on his face of – I'm not sure how to describe it – concern? Worry? Maybe even terror? Toby saw me looking at him, though, and immediately stuck out his enormous tongue at me.

Then something occurred to me.

"When's the final?" I asked Mom.

"Sunday night," she said.

No big deal, I thought. Toby probably didn't want to see me race anyway. Yes, he came along to a lot of my meets, but it was more about the hot dogs than the hot racing.

"We can all watch it in your hotel room," I said. "I'm sure Coach Sheeds will let me."

A look crossed Mom's face and she said, "But, darling."

My mum isn't really a "But, darling" sort of person, so immediately I knew something was up.

"The show is actually taped in the afternoon," she said.

"And you told Toby you'd go?" I said.

"Your dad and your grandfather will be at the race, of course," said Mom.

"Of course," I said.

"Time for dinner!" said Mom, clapping her hands. "Everybody at the table, please."

Again my stomach rumbled ominously, so I paid a visit to the bathroom, hoping something would happen.

But nothing happened. When I returned everybody was already seated and I copped another dirty look from Mom.

There was one empty seat, so I took it. Miranda was on my left. And next to her was Seb. And across the table was Tristan.

And he was giving me this weird, inane sort of smile.

I picked, supermodel style, at the food that was put in front of me. And then it was dessert time.

Dad made a little speech. About parenthood, about watching your children grow and thrive, about the joy you have in their achievements. Mom made a little speech. About parenthood, about watching your children grow and thrive, about the joy you have in their achievements.

And the ice cream came out, on a silver platter, a great glistening pyramid of it. There were "ooh"s and there were "aah"s and there was a round of applause.

"Only a little bit for me," I said to Mom, but she piled my plate high.

After the first spoonful I knew I was in trouble.

I put my spoon down, but Mom glared at me. I knew what she was thinking, too: that the green-eyed monster she'd recently been on about had reared its head.

I dug in again, bringing the loaded spoon to my mouth. My throat constricted, the ball of ice cream in my mouth had nowhere to go.

I stood up, intent on getting to the bathroom. But I was gagging. So either the ice cream extruded from my nostrils and I began to look like the soft-serve machine at McDonald's, or I opened my mouth.

I choose the latter, and after a tremendous choking sound, the ice cream flew out.

Now all eyes were on it, as it arced through the air, a milky-tailed meteor, and landed back on the plate. *Splat!*

An appalled silence followed.

Until one person spoke.

"Great shot, buddy," said Tristan.

FRONT PAGE VIEWS

The next morning, when I walked into the kitchen, I walked into Alaska, into Antarctica, into Yakutsk, officially the world's coldest city.

Mom was juicing her juice.

"Morning, Mother," I said.

She said nothing, but I knew what she was thinking: green-eyed monster, head, raise. She was thinking that I'd intentionally sabotaged Toby's big moment.

But maybe she just hadn't heard me over the grind of the juicer, I thought. So I repeated the greeting, louder this time.

"Morning," she replied, her voice glacial.

No: monster, head, raise, for sure.

"Hi, Tobes," I said to my younger brother, who was shoveling cereal into the cement mixer that was his mouth. In return I got a look that would snap-freeze a polar bear.

Again: not fair.

I looked over at Miranda. Eyes on her iPad, she was gnawing on toast.

"Morning, sis," I said.

She looked up at me and slowly shook her head. As if I was a disappointment. As if I was a lost cause.

It was a relief when Dad appeared, suited up, ready for work.

"Didn't run this morning, champ?" he said, shaking muesli into a bowl.

"Tummy's still a bit dodgy," I said, hands over stomach.

He lowered his voice. "Wasn't a good look, was it?" He poured soy milk onto his muesli. "The ice cream thing."

"Not a good look at all," I agreed.

Dad threw me a half smile, but it wasn't enough.

It was still Alaska, Antarctica, Yakutsk.

I wanted him to tell me that it was going to be all right, that The Debt would be repaid and my life would return to normal.

"Might be a just dairy thing," he said. "You could try soy."

"Sure, Dad," I said, my voice intentionally low. "Soy will really solve everything."

His spoon stopped mid-muesli and he fixed me with a look.

I know my dad's very handsome. That he has excellent hair. And he dresses well. And keeps fit. I know all that, but most of the time it seems to me that Dad is sort of bland, the way a lot of businessman types are sort of bland.

Sort of bland and sort of boring.

There was nothing bland or boring about that look he gave me, though.

It was an angry look.

And a fierce look.

Maybe even a mean look.

And it said: *Stop whining, because you're not the only one who has had to go through this crap.*

I met his look, though. And he was the first to look away, back to his stupid muesli and his stupid soy milk. But that didn't matter, that was a crap game anyway, because he'd already said, without uttering a single word, all that he needed to say.

If it'd been Yakutsk before, it was even colder now.

"Is that a whistle?" I said, though I'd heard nothing at all. "I'll go get the paper."

Outside, I made for the fig tree on our front lawn, the one that still had the remnants of a tree house, and collapsed under it.

Leaves rustled. Birds sang. Clouds chased after each other in the great blue playground of the sky.

"Hi, Dom!"

"Tristan!" I said. "You scared the crap out of me!"

"Sorry," he said, sitting down next to me.

When I say next to me, I really mean next to me: our butts were practically touching.

Look, I'm a pretty modern sort of fifteen year old, not fazed by a bit of male-on-male contact, but I couldn't help shuffling away from him a bit.

At least until there was no more butt-on-butt action happening.

And what was it with Tristan, anyway? Why was he just wandering around? Yes, I knew he didn't have to get ready for school, but still. The old Tristan never did this.

Leaves rustled. Birds sang. Clouds chased after each other ...

"Hey, Dom," said Tristan. "You know before the coma?"

"BC, you mean? Before Coma?"

"Yeah, that's right: BC. What did we used to do apart from taking the boat for a spin?"

"You seriously can't remember?"

"Hey, I'm asking, aren't I? The specialist said that sometimes, after a coma, people have trouble accessing their memory."

Like a corrupted hard disk, I thought, *whirring and whirring, looking for data that isn't there.*

"So what did we get up to, you and me, BC?"

"I don't know, the usual stuff. Hang out. Horse around. Make fun of stuff. Hang out a bit more. More horsing around. Make fun of more stuff."

A motorbike passed and the rolled up newspaper flew towards us.

I leapt up and plucked it out of the air one-handed.

"Great to talk, Tristan," I said, walking quickly towards the house.

Look, I had to admit, I wasn't a big newspaper reader.

Mostly I just looked at the sports section, mostly the athletics, mostly the running. And because there was seldom any running, mostly I read nothing.

I removed the plastic bag and was about to flick to the sports section when something on the front page caught my eye.

LAZARUS BROTHERS IMPLICATED IN LATEST GOLD COAST MURDER read the headline, and under that was a large photo of the implicated Lazarus brothers.

Behind them, sitting on a tiny wooden stool, a triple-shot espresso in hand, was yours truly.

Okay, I wasn't in focus, my face was grainy, but surely anybody who knew me would recognize it as me.

Or would they?

There was one way to find out.

I took the paper back inside, held up the front

page so Mom and Dad, both now sitting at the table, could see it.

"Check out these Lazarus brothers," I said. "They're mean-looking dudes, aren't they?"

Dad looked up from his muesli.

"Wouldn't want to meet them in a dark alley," he said.

"Don't you reckon, Mom?"

She looked up from her juice, and said, "Scum."

If my own parents didn't recognize me, then I doubted whether anybody from school would.

I figured it had to do with context: me sitting at Cozzi's at ten in the morning on a school day just wasn't what you'd expect.

I was safe, then.

Safe from the standard Grammar punishment for ditching school, which was three days' suspension. But as I put bread in the toaster, I realized that I had this wrong. Maybe three days' suspension wasn't such a bad thing. Because, let's face it, school was totally getting in the way.

And if I did get suspended Gus would have to look after me. Which pretty much meant I could do what I liked.

Yes, I had found a way to ditch, but it was complicated and it was risky and I'd already been found out.

As I ate the toast, I tried to think it through. Did

I really want to get suspended from school? By the time I'd finished my toast I knew the answer.

I went upstairs to my bedroom. Found the Lazarus brothers' photo on the net. Copied it, pasted it into Word. Wrote *Is that Dom Silvagni?* in 14 point Arial Rounded MT Bold on the bottom. I thought about emailing it but decided against it: emails can sit there unopened for yonks. But a fax, that arrives pre-opened.

Sometimes the old technology just rocks, I told myself as I WinFaxed the doctored photo to the school's fax number.

I went back downstairs.

When the home phone rang a couple of minutes later, Toby answered it.

"Mom, it's for you," he said. "It's Grammar."

Mom took the phone. As she listened to whoever it was on the other end she walked over to the kitchen table and studied the front page.

"Yes," she said. "I agree it does look a bit like him, but ..."

I interrupted. "It is me!"

"Sorry, can you hold on for a second?" said Mom, cupping her hand over the phone's mouthpiece. "It's you?"

"It's me, I totally ditched school. I pretty much

deserve any punishment they dish out," I said cheerfully.

After all the porky pies I'd been serving up lately, it actually felt really good to tell the truth.

Mom took her hand off the mouthpiece. "Dom has just owned up, Mr. Cranbrook. No, I agree absolutely." She put down the phone.

Shocked, she said, "You're suspended until next Tuesday."

I punched the air with my fist.

Which probably wasn't the best idea. Because Mom collapsed into a chair and started crying.

Or was it crying?

Was she using some of the skills that had caused the great Pacino to remark, "You've got real presence, babe"?

And Dad had reverted back to his normal bland self; he must've known that it was Debt-related.

The phone rang again.

And again Toby answered it. But this time it was for me.

"Yes, Dom speaking," I said.

"What were you thinking?"

This voice was so strident, it took me a second to work out that it was Coach Sheeds talking.

"I've just been summoned by the principal," she said. "You've gone and gotten yourself suspended!"

"The race is on Sunday," I said.

"It doesn't matter," she said. "You can't race!"

"But the race is on the weekend," I said. "Not a school day."

"You're not listening to me, Dom. You are suspended. You cannot race. You are not going to Rome."

Each word like a bullet thud-thud-thudding into the target, smashing my dreams, destroying my life.

"Dom?" said Coach. "Are you okay?"

I wanted to collapse onto the floor, I wanted to open the floodgates and let the tears come.

I wanted to, but I didn't.

"Of course I'm okay," I said, and I hung up.

LITTLE SILICON VALLEY

I checked the address again: 958 Goldman Avenue, Silicon Valley. It was an empty block. Tussocks of brown grass and piles of rubbish and a faded *For Sale* sign. So much for Dr. Chakrabarty and his cryptics, I thought. What a waste of time, of a ninety-eight-minute train trip. And had I just gone and gotten myself suspended for nothing? Missed out on the race for absolutely no reason?

But then it occurred to me: Usain Bolt actually had two world records: the 100 meters in 9.58 seconds and the 200 meters in 19.19 seconds. So I kept walking until I got to 1919 Goldman Avenue.

It looked like any other factory in the area, a big boxy building made from concrete blocks. The trees outside were spindly, gray with dust. Ragged plastic bags danced in the wind. A mangy dog sniffed about. On a wall the company's name – *ase Logi* –

was spelled out in letter cutouts. It took me a while to realize that a couple of cutouts were missing, that it should've read *Case Logic.* That was encouraging, anyway. Case, housing, they were the same thing, weren't they?

I guess I was expecting something like the Styxx Emporium, a cathedral of geek-chic. But when I thought about it, it made sense that the prototype Cerberus housing would be manufactured in such an unassuming place. Why make a big thing out of it? Why draw attention to it?

Okay, it was now time to implement the next part of my plan. All the way on the train I'd tried to come up with alternatives to what I was just about to do, and I did come up with alternatives, lots of them, but none of them was as good, or as heartbreaking. So I took my iPhone out, removed it from its skin and placed it on the ground. I picked up a rock.

"Forgive me, for I am about to sin," I said as I brought the rock down hard, crunching my iPhone.

The case cracked, the screen cracked and from the sky came several jagged bolts of lightning. Okay, I made up the last bit, but felt like I totally deserved to be mega-zapped by the great Apple god.

Crunched iPhone in hand, I walked towards the building.

All Visitors to Report to the Office said a sign, an arrow pointing around the side.

I pushed open the office door and walked inside. Again, I couldn't help but think of the Styxx Emporium. Its sleek interior, the merchandise arranged like priceless museum exhibits, shiny and spotlighted. Such a contrast to this place.

A woman sat at a desk, typing at an ancient computer. Okay, it wasn't exactly a Commodore 64, but it still looked pretty old.

"Hi," I said.

She looked up at me and said, "Deliveries are around the side, luv."

"That's not why I'm here," I said.

"It's not?" she said.

As I put my iPhone on the counter I could hardly believe what I'd done to it, and the tears that formed in my eyes were the genuine article.

"It needs a new case," I said.

The woman stood up, smoothed down her skirt.

"Oh, the poor thing," she said, looking at my iPhone as if it was an injured animal, like a juvenile bird that had dropped out of its nest and needed to be put out of its misery. "I'm not sure who sent you here, luv, but we're not a retailer."

The oh-my-poor-iPhone tears were already there, why not use them?

I screwed my eyes tight, squeezing them out.

But as I did, as they started to make their pathetic way down my cheeks, something weird happened:

other, more legitimate tears decided that they wanted out too.

Imogen-isn't-my-friend tears. I'm-not-running-at-the-nationals tears.

The floodgates were open.

The-Debt-is-going-to-take-my-leg tears.

My-life-is-broken tears.

"Oh, you poor boy," said the woman, ripping some tissues from a box and handing them to me. "I know how you feel."

"It's my sister's phone," I said. "She's got coimetrophobia."

The woman gave me a sympathetic look and some more tissues before she said, "Come on, let's have a look out back before the boss gets back from his run."

I followed her out back, into a storage area. There were rows and rows of shelves on which were square plastic containers, each containing a different type of phone housing. From the other side of a wall I could hear machine noises; I assumed that was where the actual manufacturing was done.

"It's an iPhone 5, right?" said the woman.

"Yes," I said, and I followed her down one of the rows.

She stopped and pointed to a bin that was labeled *IP5*. "Take your pick."

As I took a case from the bin, I checked out the

other bins on the shelf, the ones labeled IP, IP3 and IP4. All iPhones, I reasoned.

My eyes traveled to the shelf above. There was a bin labeled SC – the Styxx Charon? – and another labeled SP – the Styxx Phaëthon? – but the one that really caught my attention was labeled *SX*.

"What's *SX*?" I asked.

"Wouldn't have a –" she started, before she corrected herself. "No, wait, I do know. That's a special order we had."

"Can I have a look?"

"Better not, luv," she said.

I thought about just grabbing one and running for it, but I decided against it – the woman had been so nice to me.

We went back to the office and I said, "How much do I owe you?"

"Don't worry about it," she said. "A present for your poor sister."

I thanked her, went outside and scurried around the side of the building until I came to a delivery dock. There was a set of sliding doors that were slightly ajar.

A security guard was standing in front of them.

I picked up a stone, threw it at a nearby dumpster.

As I did, I thought: *Is he really going to fall for the oldest trick in the book?*

The stone hit the dumpster with a surprisingly loud *clang!*

"Hey! Who's that?" said the security guard, falling for the oldest trick in the book and making towards the dumpster.

As he did, I ran behind him and slipped through the open doors and inside.

I walked around pallets loaded with boxes until I was back in the storage area. I made for the row, and grabbed a case from the *SX* box.

A quick glance, and I knew that it was what I was after. It was bigger than an iPhone case, but much slimmer, and it was transparent.

I was just about to put it in my pocket when somebody said, "Hey, what are you doing there?"

A man was standing at the end of the row, in running gear, dripping sweat.

When the woman said that her boss was on a run I'd assumed she meant a business run, dropping off parcels, something like that. But he really had been on a run.

"Nothing," I said, looking at the case still in my hand.

"Hey –" he started, but I didn't hear the rest because I was running.

Back down the row, behind the pallets, out through the sliding doors.

The security guard, back at his post, went to grab me, but I fended him off rugby style with a straight-arm hand in the chest.

"Get him!" I heard the boss yell.

I ran back along the side of the building. When I was on the street I looked over my shoulder.

The security guard was behind me, but that was where he was going to stay – nobody with a running style as cumbersome as that was ever going to catch up to me.

I slowed down a bit to catch my breath.

As I did I, heard the scuff of footsteps.

Was the security guard foxing? Had he gone from cumbersome to Speedy Gonzales?

But when I looked behind, it was to see the boss chasing after me. Immediately, I did what all runners do when they're in a race: I analyzed my opponent's style, his form.

My conclusion: he, the boss, could run.

I better get a move on, I thought as I went up several gears. I had another problem, however: I didn't really know where I was, or where I was going. When I reached a T-junction, I turned left. This street looked the same as the previous street, the buildings looked the same as the previous buildings. I took a quick glance behind – he was still on my tail.

I thought of Coach Sheeds's Hakuna Matata. A gazelle must run faster than the fastest lion or it will be killed. A lion must run faster than the slowest gazelle or it will starve. Right now, I was a gazelle.

I increased my speed. If he was just a casual runner he wouldn't be used to that, to running in spurts, to Kenyan running. When I dropped it back down again, I looked behind. I'd put a bit more distance between us, but not a huge amount.

This guy was more than just a casual runner.

Up ahead, on my left, I saw an alley. I kicked again, veered into it. On either side were the backs of factories, dumpsters overflowing with rubbish.

Then walls. Then a high chain-link fence. The deadest of dead ends.

Nowhere to go but back.

I looked behind, and the lion was almost on me. He stopped about four meters away. Chest heaving, he was trying not to show how much he was hurting.

"You're a lovely runner," he said, between gasps.

"You're pretty good, too," I said.

"You a miler?" he said. "You look like a miler."

"Yeah," I said. "What about you?"

"Marathons," he said. "I'm in for the long haul."

He pointed at the case that was still in my hand. "You need to give that back to me, son."

"I do?" I said.

He nodded, walking towards me, hand out-stretched.

I could've charged him, tried to knock him over, maybe even hit him. Or I could've used the skills I learned in my one season of football and dodged him. But I didn't.

I handed over the case.

"Good lad," he said, smiling.

And then I ran, jumping out of the blocks like Usain Bolt.

I sprinted past him, back down the alley, back along one street. Past the security guard, bent over, gulping for air. Halfway along the next street I hit the wall: oxygen debt, lactic acid, thighs on fire, all that stuff. And I wanted to end the pain, wanted to stop.

Suddenly, I was at Stadio Olimpico in Rome, the last lap of the 1500 meters.

I've got a five-meter lead, but they're catching up: the Kenyan and the Ethiopian and the Moroccan.

The crowd is on their feet.

The crowd is roaring.

And I've got to find something, got to find some guts.

The Kenyan, the Moroccan, the Ethiopian kick as one, and so do I.

A burst of power that starts at my toes and surges through my fingertips.

I reached 1919 Goldman Avenue. Scrambled along the side of the building, in through the sliding door. Into the iPhone row. Grabbed another *SX* case.

When I was out on the street again, I saw him in the distance. Trudging along.

Marathon man, you just don't want to mess with us milers.

ANAGRAMS

All the way home I was on a high.

And why not?

I'd devised a pretty audacious plan and then I'd successfully executed that pretty audacious plan.

Even when I swapped the sim card from my damaged phone into my old iPhone 4 I was still on a high.

There was nothing wrong with an iPhone 4, I told myself: it wasn't so long ago that it was tomorrow's technology, it wasn't so long ago that it was Cerberus.

And that's just about when I fell off my high, toppling, head over toes, back to earth.

Who was I kidding?

I was only a third of the way to a whole Cerberus, and that was assuming the other two components were as accessible as this one had been.

It was time to stop slapping myself on the back and time to return to work.

I opened ClamTop, once again bringing up the session from the day we'd nabbed Nitmick.

He'd sent this email to SheikSnap@hotmail.com.

Interceded huge toys? That's so scrambled!

I remembered what Dr. Chakrabarty had said: if you see the words "crazy," "mixed-up" or "scrambled," then you pretty much know it's an anagram.

So I did what he'd done: I wrote the letters that made up *Interceded huge toys?* in a circle and tried to find something that made sense.

It was easy to find words, but I couldn't use all the letters up and make a meaningful phrase or sentence.

Something occurred to me. I got on my computer, typed *anagram* into Google. The first hit was called Anagram Server, a "free web-based anagram generator."

See, Miranda, Google is my friend!

I went to this website, entered *interceded huge toys* into the field and hit enter.

I got 55,557 results!

I started scrolling through them, starting with *ceded tighteners you*. After about ten minutes, I was ready to give up but then I found it: *did you get the screen*.

That had to be it.

I went to SheikSnap@hotmail.com's reply.

It consisted of a single symbol: *!*

There was only one conclusion: SheikSnap@hotmail.com, whoever they were, already had the screen.

Now all I had to do was find out who SheikSnap@hotmail.com was.

And get the screen from them.

I typed three words into the anagram server. The website took about a second to generate two hundred and sixty-six anagrams.

After looking through them all I decided on *see nice nerd*.

So far so good, but now I was into more technical territory, like how in the blazes did you phish somebody?

But then I remembered that the program Guzman had used to phish Nitmick had been called Nuclear Phishing.

Easy, I assured myself. I'd just download myself a little old copy of Nuclear Phishing.

I entered that as a search string into Google and hit enter and all I got was a whole lot of stuff about the evils of phishing.

I thought of what Miranda said, that Google censored results.

Maybe she was right.

Hey, but Google wasn't the only search engine out there!

So I tried Bing, Yahoo, AltVista, Webcrawler, Lycos and DogPile.

And I still got nada.

So I went down to the kitchen and filled a bowl right to the top with chocolate ice cream and poured chocolate topping over that and sprinkled that with chocolate chips and came back upstairs.

If there's anybody who thinks chocolate isn't brain food, then they're a total cretin.

Because after I'd finished the chocolate ice cream with chocolate topping and chocolate chips it came to me: I was going about this the totally wrong way.

If you want some dirty work done, then you need a dirty worker.

Which Google obviously wasn't. And neither was Bing. Or Lycos. None of those Goody Two-shoes search engines.

But which one was?

I vaguely remembered these nerdy kids at school talking about something called Astalavista.

Astalavista was easy to find, which was a bit of a worry – surely something so evil should be more hidden.

Its tag, "the best underground download portal," was pretty encouraging, though.

And when I entered *Nuclear Phishing*, I got none of that righteous stuff about how bad phishing was, all I got was – hallelujah! – about a thousand different places where I could download this software.

Which I proceeded to do.

After installing the program, I typed Nitmick's email address into the "From email:" field. Typed *SheikSnap@hotmail.com* into the "To email:" field. I typed *hey did you "see nice nerd," he was totally mixed up* into the message section and hit send.

Now it was a waiting game: it could be hours, days, weeks until I got a reply.

Or if they were on to me, then there wouldn't be any reply at all, except maybe one that consisted of two monosyllabic words.

But I got a reply almost instantaneously: *coca fizzes*.

I didn't need an anagram server for this – it had to be Cozzi's Café.

I replied straightaway with an emoticon: ☺

And received one in return: ☺

Now? I wrote.

Hero union, came the reply: in one hour.

One hour was perfect because a plan was forming in my head, a plan that necessitated quite a few phone calls.

Firstly to the dubious Hound and then, hopefully, to some of his even more dubious acquaintances.

When I'd managed to do this I went to go downstairs.

From the top of the stairs I could see Gus sitting

at the kitchen table, staring into the distance.

For some reason he'd taken his prosthetic off and it was just lying on the floor next to him.

I stopped and watched.

Gus didn't move, just kept staring.

That was so unlike him, because Gus was always doing something: reading, writing notes, lifting weights, something.

I felt a chill.

Okay, Gus was old, but he was so fit, so strong, so active, I never really thought of him as being old old.

But right then, he looked exactly that, old old, like somebody who had had enough.

I wondered if me not being allowed to race in the nationals had anything to do with it. Gus hadn't said much beyond "Blazing bells and buckets of blood" but it seemed that he had changed somehow.

I took another step, making sure I scuffed my shoes so he knew I was coming.

Immediately, he turned his attention to the book that was open on the table.

"Hey, I just have to pop out for a while," I said.

"I promised your mum that I'd make sure you stayed put," said Gus.

I gave him a look and it was enough.

"Okay, I didn't see you go," he said as I made for the door. "You sneaked totally out of the window."

"Thanks," I said. "And actually it's 'totally

sneaked,' not 'sneaked totally.'"

"Okay, you totally sneaked out of the window."

"Totally, dude," I said as I opened the door.

COZZI'S AGAIN

As soon as I got there I realized that this was a really tricky place to meet. Especially at this hour as there were so many people dropping in after work. How was I supposed to know which one of them was SheikSnap@hotmail.com?

I went inside the café, got in line. It was the same stubbly man serving, he of the "Either you order a real coffee or you go to Starbucks" line.

Except he didn't call it Starbucks.

Immediately, I had another cause to be concerned. Humiliation, I reckoned, must have a half-life somewhere between Uranium and Plutonium. I started practicing my order in my head: *an espresso please, an espresso please.*

In front of me was a girl who looked like Miranda – she was about the same age, had the same degree of emo-nality. She was even carrying an iBag, just like Miranda usually did. I felt a rush of excitement: could this be SheikSnap?

When it was her turn to be served she said, "I'll have a soy dandelion."

No! I thought.

"Either you order a real coffee or you go to Starbucks," he said.

Except he didn't call it Starbucks.

Well, at least he was an equal-opportunity a-hole.

The girl gave him an emo death stare before she said, "Do you know I could tweet saying I saw a cockroach in your coffee grinder and I guarantee you in an hour it would be on thousands of other tweets and furthermore just about everybody who read it would believe it?"

Wow! Why couldn't I have come up with something like that?

And more wow! She was sounding more and more like a candidate for SheikSnap.

The man glared at her for a while before he said, "We have some lovely tea made with fresh mint. Would you like some of that?"

"That'd be awesome, dude," said the girl.

"Yes?" he barked at me when it was my turn.

After all that practice, I still got it wrong.

"The usual," I said.

He looked at me, narrowing his eyes.

What an idiot I am, I thought. *I've only been here once before.*

"Triple espresso then?" he said.

"That's right," I said.

"Take a seat, Snake'll find you," he said before he called the order out to the barista.

I went outside, and found a seat near where emo girl was reading the newspaper. I did a quick head count. Besides her, there were twenty-two people spread along the pavement. And not one of them was obviously a nerd, let alone a criminal nerd, the sort of person who would be friends with Nitmick.

She had to be SheikSnap@hotmail.com.

Snake arrived with my coffee.

"The Triplicate Kid," he said, handing it to me.

His boots looked even pointier, his jeans even tighter than last time I was here. And he was wearing the same retro fanny pack.

No caffeine now or I'll be up all night, I decided, so I put the cup on a table in front of me.

But Snake just stood there, looking at me.

I felt I had no choice – I picked the coffee up, took a sip. Again that explosion in my mouth.

"Wow!" I said.

Satisfied, Snake moved on.

"Sorry, do you have a pen?"

It was the emo girl.

"Somewhere," I said, and patted my pockets until I found it.

I handed it to her.

"Thanks," she said. "I won't be long."

She folded the paper over and started on the crossword. The cryptic.

Hand flying, she quickly filled in the blanks, but she seemed to get stumped on the last clue.

It has to be her. It just has to be!

The emo girl looked at her watch, brought out her Galaxy. She was about to make a call when she seemed to change her mind.

"Can you mind my seat?" she said. "I need to go to the ladies."

"Sure," I said.

I watched as she made her way back along the footpath, but instead of turning into the café where the ladies was, she kept walking until she came to a public phone, one of the few left on the Coast. She fed the machine some money. Made a call. When she'd finished, she came back.

"Thanks," she said as she sat back down in her seat.

I had no doubt now: it was her. Nitmick hadn't turned up, so she'd tried to call him. And just like crims the world over, she'd resorted to the anonymity of the public phone. Still, it was better to make absolutely sure before I put my plan into action.

"Must be contagious," I said. "I have to go now."

"No problem," she said. "I've got your back."

I walked back along the footpath. Because I wasn't sure if she was looking at me or not, I turned into the café. Walked past the bathrooms and out through the back door and into an alley. Along the alley, out onto a cross street. When I got to the intersection I had a peep around the corner. SheikSnap was engrossed in her Galaxy. I hurried over to the public phone, shoved a coin into the slot and hit redial.

The phone rang and then a man said, "Yeah?"

He didn't sound like Nitmick, but who knew what voice-altering techno gadgetry somebody as paranoid as him would use?

So I said, "Nitmick?"

The man said, his voice a low rumble, "Look, you after something or not?"

"What you got?" I said.

"Go-ey, e's, oxies – the usual."

I hung up.

SheikSnap wasn't SheikSnap after all – she was just some soy-loving emo who was waiting for her drug dealer to turn up.

I went in through the back door of the café and out through the front.

"Thanks," I said to her as I sat down.

She was still engrossed in the crossword.

Snake snaked past, empty coffee cups up each arm.

"What's the clue?" he said to the former SheikSnap.

"Returned beer, fit for king," said the former SheikSnap. "The last letter is –"

But before she had a chance to say what this last letter was Snake said, "Regal."

"Regal?"

"Sure, beer is lager, and 'lager' returned is 'regal.'"

"Very good," said the former SheikSnap, smiling, as she set about filling in the missing letters.

When she'd finished she handed me my pen.

Could Snake be SheikSnap?

The answer to that question came very soon afterwards.

"Hey, Snake Hips!" somebody nearby said.

So Snake's full name was Snake Hips.

I wrote *Snake Hips* on my hand and crossed out the letters one by one. First *s*, then *h* then *e* then *i* and so on.

When I'd finished there were no spare letters – SheikSnap was an anagram of Snake Hips!

I took out my iPhone, sent a text.

Ten minutes later and a woman appeared. Her face was hidden by a headscarf and a pair of enormous sunglasses, and she was trying to negotiate a stroller through the jumble of stools and people towards where Snake was serving some customers.

Getting more and more frustrated, she gave the stroller a shove, and somehow it toppled over, its swaddled contents rolling out onto the pavement.

Ohmigod!

I got to my feet.

But Snake had already put down the coffee he was serving and was rushing over.

He went to pick the baby up, but the mother screeched, "Don't touch my baby," and pushed him over.

And then somebody else got involved, barreling into Snake. Eventually the woman shoved the baby back into the stroller, and she and the other person hurried off.

"My bag!" said Snake, getting up from the ground, feeling around his waist. "Somebody took my bag!"

Ω   Ω   Ω

They were exactly where they said they'd be: in the alley behind the fire station, sharing a cigarette.

"So you got it?" I said.

PJ reached into the stroller and brought out Snake's fanny pack.

"Is the baby okay?" I said.

"Bubby's okay?" cooed Brandon, taking the baby from the stroller and casually tossing it in my direction.

I went to catch it but I missed, and the baby bounced on the ground. I rushed over and picked it up. The baby had glassy eyes. Dirty pink skin. And a little hole for a mouth.

"It's a doll!" I said.

This cracked Brandon up – he opened his mouth and laughter spilled out. But the laughter soon turned into a cough, and the cough turned into something that Brandon dredged out of his lungs and hacked onto the ground.

"Charming," I said, again thinking of that Neil Young song: "Needle and the Damage Done."

PJ threw me an *I'm sorry* look as she handed me the fanny pack.

I unzipped the bag. There was a Styxx Charon in there, and something else, wrapped in Bubble Wrap. I held it up to the light. It was a screen, and it looked exactly the right size for the housing.

I reached into my pocket, brought out a wad of cash and held it out to PJ.

"Hey, half that's mine!" said Brandon, moving towards her, snatching at the money.

"Your boyfriend's got lovely manners," I said to PJ.

"Look who's talking," said PJ, eyes flashing.

Okay, she had a point, and a pretty good one. Arranging to get somebody's bag stolen probably wasn't something they'd teach you at finishing school.

I shrugged my shoulders and got one of her trademark winks in return.

"And he's not my boyfriend," she said.

I'm not sure why I was pleased to hear this – what

did I care if some street kid had a boyfriend or not? But I was.

But if he wasn't her boyfriend, why did they hang out together?

My question wasn't a question for long.

"Come on, sis, give me my share," said Brandon.

"Not until we see your doctor," said PJ, moving off, away from her brother.

He hurried after her.

And I moved away in the opposite direction.

FIRE IN THE FACTORY

When a taxi approached, I put out my arm.

It stopped, and I took a quick look inside. Was it the same taxi that had kidnapped me? Hard to tell; all taxis look pretty much the same.

"Dominic," said the driver, but with the stress on the last syllable. *Dom-i-NIC.*

Taxi, accent: it's Luiz Antonio, I thought. *He must be driving for a different company now.*

I looked closer at him.

No, it wasn't Luiz Antonio. And although he appeared sort of familiar, I wasn't sure who he was. He soon helped me with that, though.

"I am father of Rashid," he said in faltering English.

"Nice to meet you," I said.

"I have watched you running many times," said Father of Rashid. "You are very fast."

Now I had another dilemma: front seat or backseat? Front seat would mean that, inevitably, I'd have to engage with Father of Rashid. And after what I'd just been through, I didn't want to engage with anybody. But if I got into the backseat, would Father of Rashid be insulted? I mean, he was the father of my schoolmate, my teammate. I knew that strategically it was a dumb thing to do, but I couldn't help myself, I got into the front seat, and told Father of Rashid that I wanted to go to Halcyon Grove.

"Do you mind if I have news radio on?" he said. "Good for my English." *Engleesh*.

"No," I said. "Of course not."

"*An extensive search is now underway for two teenagers caught by a flash flood in a storm water drain and believed to be washed out to sea,*" said the reporter.

Poor buggers, I thought, as I slumped back, closing my eyes.

The taxi had barely started moving before Father of Rashid started engaging the crap out of me.

"Your best time for race of fifteen hundred is four minute one seconds and forty," he said.

"Yes," I said, astonished that he knew this.

"My son Rashid is four minute five second and twenty-two," he said.

"That's a great time."

"Good time, not great time," he said. "Rashid race with heart not head."

He was right there because Rashid was a compulsive front-runner, he couldn't wait to get out in the lead. Front-running was spectacular, front-running was exhilarating, but front-running seldom got gold.

Father of Rashid didn't have very good English, but that didn't mean he was reluctant to use it. He knew an amazing amount of stuff about running, the track team, about the school.

Then I heard, *"There was a fire in a factory in Little Silicon Valley this morning."*

"Can you please turn the volume up?" I asked Father of Rashid.

"The factory, which supplied components for the electronics industry, was completely destroyed," said the reporter.

Could it be the same factory? A possible scenario immediately came to mind: start a fire and in the ensuing confusion, with all that smoke, sneak in and steal a case. Crude but effective.

It had to be the same factory!

I thought of the owner, the marathoner. He didn't deserve to have his factory destroyed like that.

When we pulled up at the entrance to Halcyon Grove Father of Rashid said, "That Bevan Milne, he's perhaps a bit of a turd?"

I couldn't help but agree. "Yes, perhaps a bit of a turd."

Ω Ω Ω

When I walked into the house Gus and Tristan were sitting at the kitchen table, playing chess.

Tristan!

What was he doing in my house? And what was he doing playing chess with my grandfather?

"Your gramps sure is one smart old dude," said Tristan.

"Not so sure about that," said Gus, looking up from the game, his eyes traveling from one end of my body to the other, as if he was doing some sort of mental inventory: head – tick; both arms – tick; both legs – tick.

Look, chess isn't exactly my thing, but it looked like Tristan was giving my gramps a run for his money.

"I'll leave you two to your game," I said. "I'm going for a run on Dad's treadmill."

Actually, I wanted to watch Fox News, see if there was any more information about the fire in Little Silicon Valley, but I also wanted to go for a run – okay, I wasn't going to Rome but I was still a runner.

The treadmill was, as usual, annoyingly familiar.

"Hi, Champ! Ready for a great workout?"

"Whatever, Treadmill," I said.

It was business news, all Hang Seng and Dow Jones and FTSE.

It was so boring and I wondered how Dad could possibly get excited by this stuff, how he'd gone from paying back The Debt to the All Ordinaries.

But then it occurred to me: maybe he had no choice. By the time he'd paid that sixth installment he'd used up his quota of excitement and boring was all that he had left.

Finally Fox News got around to the fire in Little Silicon Valley.

There was a factory and there was billowing smoke and there was helmeted firefighters with hoses spurting arcs of water.

"This factory on Griffin Avenue manufactured specialized circuit boards," said the reporter. *"Which means that the smoke you see behind me is potentially toxic."*

It's not my factory, it's not Case Logic! I told myself.

I felt a sense of relief – so the marathoner hadn't had his factory destroyed. Then it took me a while to sort the rest of this out in my head.

It couldn't be a coincidence.

I remembered the emails the three of them had exchanged, how they were each going to get a component.

If Nitmick had been assigned the case, and if Snake aka SheikSnap had been assigned the screen, then it followed that LoverOfLinux must have been assigned the circuit board.

Not only that, he – or she – now had the circuit board, the third ingredient!

I had the other two.

So all I needed to do now was get the circuit board off him – or her – and I had Nitmick's apple pie, I had the Cerberus.

Excitement rising, I jumped off the treadmill.

"Great run! Champ! But you haven't reached your programmed goals yet!"

"Love to stay and, like, chat, Treadmill. But some of us have work to do."

A PHISHING TRIP

Back in my room, both ClamTop and my laptop open on my desk, I powered up Snake's Charon.

The screen flashed to life.

And then it wanted a password.

Good, I thought. I couldn't get into it.

Good, I thought, I'd work out another way to find out who LoverOfLinux was that didn't involve breaking into somebody's phone, most probably stealing their identity.

That particular line would remain uncrossed.

Seriously, who was I kidding?

I'd phished Snake, I'd gone for day trips into Imogen's laptop, I'd already crossed that line over and over again.

But here I was getting all cyber-moral – what was going on?

I stuck a microUSB cable in the Charon and plugged it into the USB port on my laptop.

The usual *Please wait while drivers are being installed* ... appeared on the screen, but then – hey presto! – my machine recognized the Charon.

I powered up ClamTop.

Brought up all the local networks.

I didn't feel so guilty hacking into SILVAGNINET – I mean, it was our network at home.

But as I watched ClamTop run a series of commands, as I watched it crack the password on Snake's phone like a walnut, I could feel it, the guilt, creeping up on me.

Get over it, Dom! I told myself. *We live in the age of identity theft: it's no big deal.*

I cloned the Charon's home screen.

I didn't know that much about Styxx phones, but when five minutes later a little window popped up I figured it was from some sort of IM app.

Hi Snake Hips, where you been? somebody by the name of Angie had written.

I thought about replying, attempting to extract some information from Angie, but I was interrupted by a knock on my door.

"Go away," I said.

"There's somebody here to see you," said Miranda.

"Then you can tell them to go away too," I said.

"It's me," came a voice, Imogen's voice.

I jumped up and opened the door and she was standing there, wearing a dress with flowers all over it.

"Imogen," I said, the three syllables slipping off my tongue.

Miranda melted away so it was just the two of us.

"Can I come in?"

"Sure." I took a quick glance at the ClamTop's screen, at the cloned Charon. "Your mum ...?" I said, stumbling over my words.

"I'm getting pretty good at sneaking out," she said.

Imogen had been in my room countless times, playing on the computer, doing homework, just hanging out, but now I felt so awkward, like in the whole room there weren't two spots where we could be comfortable with each other.

So I stood near the desk and Imogen stood under the poster of Sebastian Coe winning Olympic gold.

Imogen looked at me. I looked at Imogen. There was a whole lot of looking but not much talking going on.

Until Imogen eventually said, "I heard you're not allowed to run at the nationals."

"You did?"

"Yes. I'm so sorry about that, Dom."

"So am I," I said.

I realized that I'd been so busy with The Debt that I hadn't allowed myself time to think how sorry I was.

But now Imogen, somehow, had given me permission.

And the enormity of it – I wasn't running at the nationals! – was like somebody had rammed a hose down my throat and sucked all my insides up.

I slumped into the chair and my eyes were wet.

"Dom?" said Imogen. "Are you okay?"

"Yes," I said, but my eyes were more than just wet now.

They were fountains of wetness.

I wasn't running at the nationals!

Then Imogen was next to me and her arms were around me and I could smell her smell and feel the soft fabric of her flowery dress.

My face was next to her face.

And her lips were on my lips.

We were kissing.

And then she quickly drew away.

Leaving me on another planet, in another solar system, light years away.

"We need to talk, Dom," she said.

The sound of her voice brought me back to earth, back to my room.

But I couldn't speak; all I could think of was that kiss, the taste of it as it lingered on my lips.

"I said we need to talk, Dom," said Imogen, from where she had retreated, back under Sebastian Coe.

Her voice managed to find a way through to my head.

Actually, Im, I've been trying to talk to you for

weeks. But I wasn't going to bring that up right now.

"About Tristan's pool?" I said tentatively.

"About everything."

About everything?

"There's something going on with you, Dom," she said.

"Hey, I'm fifteen. It's when the test … the test … you know, that male hormone stuff totally kicks in."

Imogen just shook her head. "You're not going to tell me, are you?"

It was my turn to shake my head. *No, I'm not. No, I can't.*

"But please still be my friend," I said. "Please, Imogen."

Behind her shoulder, another IM box popped up on ClamTop.

This one was from Fred.

I got it! he'd written.

It has to be him, I thought, excitement mounting. *This has to be LoverOfLinux.*

My eyes moved from the screen to Imogen in her dress of flowers. To the Imogen I had just kissed.

She had this look on her face, like she wanted to understand, to help.

My eyes were dragged back to the screen, to *I got it!*

"Sorry, Imogen, but I really need to get this,"

I said, pointing to the computer.

"You're impossible!" she said, and turned around and walked out, slamming the door behind her.

I jumped back in front of ClamTop and typed in *i saw the news*.

Fred answered *meet tonight at usual place*.

Now I had a problem. Obviously I – Snake Hips – knew where the usual place was. Obviously I – Dom – wouldn't have the foggiest.

I typed in *too dangerous let's go somewhere else*.

When Fred took a while to answer I guessed that he – or she – was probably suspicious.

When the reply was *saw drops?* I quit guessing: he – or she – was definitely suspicious.

It took me no time to work out that *saw drops?* was *password?*

Obviously they'd agreed on some sort of predetermined code when things got suspicious.

But what could this password possibly be?

Apple pie, I thought, remembering the conversation I'd had with Nitmick at the urinal. It just had to be apple pie.

I typed in *apple pie* and Fred disappeared.

I waited for a while, hoping that his phone had dropped out and he'd be back online soon.

But my wait was in vain.

I'd lost him.

TRACE ELEMENTS

"I'm out this morning, but Gus is coming across," said Mom the next day at breakfast.

I hadn't really slept last night. My mind had been like a storm water drain. Ideas hadn't stopped pouring into it: how to find LoverOfLinux. But they were cigarette butts, they were ice cream sticks, they were twigs, they were leaves; these ideas were rubbish.

And now it was Saturday, the day of Anna's birthday. The clock was ticking, and ticking very loudly.

To run or not to run? In the end I decided it wouldn't be such a bad idea; maybe it would clear some of the detritus from my head.

"I'm going for a run, I'll be back soon," I told Mom.

I took the usual route down Chirp Street, through Chevron Heights, up the Gut Buster, along the edge of Preacher's Forest.

As I passed the main entrance I slowed.

I couldn't really say that I liked Preacher's Forest, that it was the sort of place I'd go for a picnic, but big things had happened to me there: it's where I got tranquilized, it's where I drowned the stolen scooter, it's where the Zolt landed the plane.

And right then I was feeling desperate.

The third installment, which had had so much momentum, had come to a standstill. I needed to kick-start it, and soon.

I ran through the entrance, took the main path to the lake.

Despite it being a beautiful morning, there weren't many people around. And even those people were on mountain bikes.

So when I caught sight of the back of two figures on my left, I probably paid them a little more attention than I usually would.

And when I realized that I knew them – it was Brandon and his sister PJ – I paid them even more attention.

What were they doing here?

They were street kids, not park kids.

I wouldn't say I was actually stalking them, but I did change my direction slightly so as to keep them in sight.

And when, suddenly, they disappeared from sight, I was in equal parts surprised and intrigued.

Had they known I was behind them, had they intentionally given me the slip?

I kept running and it soon became obvious where they'd gone.

A large metal grate had been removed, giving access to a storm water pipe.

Although the pipe was enormous, at least two meters in diameter, there was absolutely no sign of water.

Did they live down there? I'd heard of people sleeping in the drains. And I remembered those two kids who'd been washed out to sea, their bodies never found. There wasn't much more to do except file that pretty useless piece of information away – *Brandon and PJ possibly live in storm water drain* – and keep moving.

When I came to the lake I sat down on a dilapidated bench. As I watched a duck make its way across the lake's surface, its wake a perfect vee, I could hear the Preacher in the distance, ranting.

Even when the Preacher and his ranting got closer I didn't move.

Even when I could see him shuffling towards me I didn't move.

I needed stuff to happen, I needed to kick-start this installment.

The Preacher stopped about a meter away from the bench, all tangled hair and crazy eyes and a smell that would drop a possum.

"And everyone that was in distress, and everyone that was in debt, and everyone that was discontented, gathered themselves unto him!" he said, his voice like a wild animal straining at its leash.

In distress? In debt? That was discontented?

Surely it couldn't be a coincidence that he was saying this stuff to me?

"What do you mean?" I said.

He stared at me, and it was as though this was the first time I'd ever really seen him. I mean beyond the hair, and beyond the dirt, beyond all the Preacher craziness.

When I saw him like this, he looked familiar. But more than that, he felt familiar. Almost like he was somebody I could trust.

He kept staring, and he opened his mouth, and he was going to say something.

But the mouth closed, no words came out, and he shuffled off.

I watched him disappear, before turning my attention back to the lake. The duck had disappeared into some reeds, but its wake was still visible, rippling outwards.

I could understand why Fred had used IM to contact Snake.

As its name suggested, it was instant, it was transitory, it was real time.

But did that mean it left no trace?

Of course not!

As I was quickly learning, everything you do on a computer leaves a trace. A program will rearrange some bytes, but often, when it's finished, it won't bother putting them back again.

And at the time Fred sent an IM to Snake's phone, ClamTop was connected to the Network.

Which meant it would've recorded the session.

Which meant the trail hadn't gone cold at all!

Surely there would be the name of the IM client, the DNS, something which would help me to work out who Fred, lover of Linux, was.

Excited, energized by this revelation, I bounced off the bench and ran at full clip all the way back to Halcyon Grove.

As I entered through the gates, a yellow-and-blue courier van exited, turning onto the main road.

Nothing unusual in that: the residents of Halcyon Grove were always getting stuff couriered to them, especially people like Mrs. Havilland who weren't that keen on going outside.

Gus and Tristan were sitting at the dining table, setting up the chess pieces.

"Don't you have a home to go to?" I said to Tristan.

Gus glared at me.

But I was in no mood to be nice.

Nice was before The Debt.

"Oh yeah, bud," said Tristan. "A courier came to pick that stuff up."

"What stuff?" I said, but already I could feel the dread: its bony fingers around my throat, it was already squeezing.

Gus shrugged. "I was late getting here."

I took the stairs two at a time. Burst into my bedroom. Snake's Charon had gone. So had the case. So had the screen.

Fred, LoverOfLinux, had done exactly what I was going to do, but he'd done it first.

I rushed downstairs, grabbed two great handfuls of Tristan's T-shirt.

"You let them go into my bedroom?" I said, shaking him hard. "What were you thinking, you idiot?"

Gus clamped me by the wrists, squeezed until I released my grip.

"I didn't," said Tristan. "It's just that there were two of them, and they had these forms, and I didn't see where they went."

"Two couriers!" I yelled. "When are there ever two couriers?"

"Leave him alone," said Gus. "It's my fault."

I looked at him, at the it's-my-fault look all over his face, and I realized that he was right – it wasn't Tristan's fault at all. If Gus had been here, like he was supposed to have been here, then none of this would've happened.

Gus wasn't wearing his prosthetic, and his stump poked out from the material of his shorts. Right then I hated Stumpy, hated this eyeless alien from a C-grade sci-fi movie more than I'd ever hated him.

"No wonder you couldn't repay The Debt," I said to my grandfather.

As soon as the words were out I wanted them back.

And I was about to say something to Gus, to apologize, when my phone rang.

It was Hound.

"If it isn't the Puppy Dog," I said, feeling kind of reckless now. I mean, could it get any worse?

"You've got until midnight," said Hound.

"Midnight to do what?"

"Get me that dirt on Guzman."

"Or what?" I said. "What are you going to do to me, Puppy Dog?"

It took Hound a while to answer and when he did there was ice in his voice.

"Do you know what I think would be really, really difficult?"

"No," I said wearily.

I just wanted to go to bed, pull the covers over my head and sleep until this was all over.

"I reckon it would be really, really difficult to

205

make ice cream if you had ten broken fingers," he said. "You know, with all that whisking they do."

There was ice in his voice and now there was ice in my guts.

Hound continued. "Especially that green tea and lychee ice cream. A heck of a lot of whisking in something like that."

He hung up and it was like the terrible threat he'd made was still in the room, filling the room, squeezing me.

He was bluffing, he had to be. Besides, I had no time to snoop on Guzman, not with the installment due today, that clock ticking so insistently.

But what if he wasn't, what if he really intended to break all my little brother's fingers?

I just couldn't allow my brother's life to be ruined because of me and my incompetence.

Something else occurred to me as well: that Guzman was somehow involved with Nitmick and his scheme. On the day we nabbed Nitmick I had the sense that he and Guzman knew each other well. And I knew that Guzman frequented Cozzi's, so there was the Snake connection.

Hound was right, it was time to get the dirt on Guzman!

"Everything okay?" said Tristan. He was sitting there, a bewildered look on his face. And Gus had gone.

"It's not, actually," I said as I bolted for the stairs.

Ω Ω Ω

I guess if there was one good thing that had come out of The Debt it was that I'd acquired a whole new skill set.

Unfortunately, phone tapping wasn't yet part of it.

Good old ClamTop, I thought.

ClamTop was going to come to my rescue yet again.

Except it didn't.

With it, I could break into networks. With it, I could clone computers. But I couldn't see any way to tap Guzman's phone.

How then?

I did some googling but couldn't find what I needed: a Dummy's Guide to Phone Tapping.

I tried Astalavista.

There was some software called PhoneSpy that look pretty promising, but when I downloaded it, my antivirus program went berserk; it was just one seething mass of Trojan viruses.

I deleted it, and leaned back in my chair.

Where to from here?

Where to from here?

I was just about to go downstairs for some brain food when I had it, a moment that was half d'oh! –

of course – and half derr! – why hadn't I thought of that before?

I'd already had my own phone tapped.

Four times!

By Zoe.

By Hound.

By the federal police.

And by Cameron Jamison.

All I had to do was exactly what they had done.

Zoe had sent me a SMS which I'd unknowingly opened, inadvertently loading spyware onto my phone.

Nice, but I just didn't think that somebody as tech savvy as Guzman was going to be as dumb as I'd been. And if I tried this, and he found out I'd tried it, he'd be even more on his guard.

No, that wouldn't work.

The federal police were part of the federal government, which meant that they obviously had a few more resources at their disposal than I did. Like the army. The navy. The SAS.

So that left Hound and Cameron Jamison.

According to Miranda, Hound had used something called an "IMSI-catcher" to monitor my calls.

And I remembered that day on Reverie Island, all that hi-tech equipment he'd had in his Hummer.

Easy, I thought, and I could feel the relief, like caffeine, hitting all the right places in my central nervous system.

I'd just borrow Hound's IMSI-catcher – how easy was that? I was working for him, after all.

So I sent him a text: *need to borrow imsi-catcher*.

The reply came back within seconds: *don't know what you're talking about*.

That was weird, I thought, but when I pondered it a bit longer it didn't seem so weird.

Maybe Hound thought his text messages were being monitored.

Maybe Hound didn't even have an IMSI-catcher.

Maybe Hound just wanted to test me.

Maybe he was telling the truth!

Whatever the answer, it seemed pretty obvious that I had to get my own IMSI-catcher.

Some further googling revealed that, surprising enough, there were spy shops where you could actually buy one.

There was a model called IMSI Snaffler.

A model called the Tactical GSM Interceptor.

And another one called Guardian Identity Catcher.

All of them, as far as I could gather, would be perfect for what I wanted.

But there was only one problem: all these spy shops that sold the IMSI-catchers were in the UK.

And when I went to the site of an Australian spy shop and entered *imsi-catcher* or even just *imsi* into the site's search field, I got absolutely no results.

Obviously, it was illegal to sell an IMSI-catcher in Australia.

Which sort of made sense.

But did that mean that the spy shops didn't sell them under the counter?

There was only one way to find out.

SPY SHOP

Will Goodes and Matt Robertson, two kids at school, had been raving about this totally awesome new spy shop that had opened up in Surfers.

"It's got a camera in a Coke can!" said Will Goodes.

"It's got a voice recorder in a watch!" said Matt Robertson.

"Yeah, whatever," said another kid. "And what possible use would you have for those?"

Plenty of possible uses, I'd thought at the time.

I'd promised myself that I'd go check it out, this totally awesome new spy shop, but I hadn't gotten around to it yet.

Not until now.

Getting there involved two bus rides.

The first was uneventful, the usual kid-takes-a-bus scenario: kid gets on bus, kid buys ticket, kid finds a seat, kid gets off bus.

But on the second bus, as I sat near the back, further researching IMSI-catchers on my iPhone, two older kids sat in front of me.

They were tough kids, tough-as kids, who had their tough-kid status written all over them: tough-kid clothes, tough-kid faces, and when the taller of the two talked, it was in a tough-kid voice.

"Grammar boy," he said.

"Actually, I'm currently on suspension from that particular institution," I said, eyes moving from my iPhone, looking the tough kid right in his tough-kid eyes.

This tough kid exchanged a glance with the other tough kid: *This one's got some attitude. Which means it'll be even more fun when we smash him into a thousand little pieces.*

"Let's have a squiz at that phone," said the other tough kid, holding out his hand.

I knew that if I handed him my iPhone I would never see it again.

"That's probably not a good idea," I said.

Before The Debt I probably would've done as they'd asked: handed them my iPhone.

And then I would've gone home, told my parents what had happened and they would've told me that I'd done exactly the right thing – why risking getting hurt? – and bought me a new one.

But that was before The Debt.

Again the tough kids exchanged tough-kid looks.

It was time to go on the attack.

"If you two don't get out of my face right now, your miserable lives are going to get a whole lot more miserable," I said.

Again the exchange of looks, but I could see a tiny flicker of doubt on the face of the tough kid.

Only tiny, but tiny was enough.

I shifted my gaze to him.

"You've got exactly one minute," I said, checking my watch. "Starting from now."

"He's full of crap," said the other tough kid to his mate.

For a second his mate was lost: which story to believe: mine or the other tough kid's?

I said nothing, just let a sort of half smile play upon my lips.

The tough kid shifted his weight and I knew I had him.

"This is stupid," he said, getting out of his seat.

The other tough kid glared at me.

"You'll keep," he said, before he, too, got up.

Next stop I got off.

The shop was situated in an arcade that housed a pawn shop and a hydroponics shop and a couple of "adult" shops and a shop that didn't really seem to sell anything.

In this setting the brand-new Surfers Spy Shop looked a bit incongruous and I wondered why they hadn't put it somewhere nicer.

As soon as I walked in, a neat-looking man with a ponytail said, his accent one hundred percent Kiwi, "By all means take a look around but no touching anything, okay?"

"Sure, bru," I replied.

"One more thing," said the man.

"Yes?"

"Can you go easy with the 'bru' thing?"

"Okay," I said.

I did exactly as he requested, taking a good look around but not touching anything.

Will Goodes and Matt Robertson were right: it was totally awesome.

I'd seen a lot of this hardware online but it was very different seeing it in the flesh.

There was nothing that resembled an IMSI-catcher, though. And I wondered how I could possibly broach the subject with the owner, who was now on the phone.

"Yes, we currently do have the MorphVoc Three in stock," he said, but I didn't really hear what else he said because my mind was now in whirl mode.

It had to be the same voice modulator that I'd done some research on during the first installment.

Now what did I know about it? Something, anything, as a conversation starter.

"Is that the Bluetooth model?" I asked after he'd hung up.

"No, there is no Bluetooth model," he said, and I felt about the same size as one of those figures you get in a McDonald's Happy Meal.

"No, wait, I tell a lie," he said. "They did release a Bluetooth, didn't they? It wasn't up to scratch, so I decided not to stock it." He flashed me a smile and said, "You know your stuff, eh?"

I shrugged, but the conversation was well and truly started.

We talked some more about hardware, but as we did I made sure I kept in role – I was just this nerdy kid who was into spy stuff.

Not this un-nerdy kid who actually used it.

The Kiwi – whose name was Hanley – told me a bit about himself.

He'd been one of those kids who needed to know how a Walkman worked. So he'd take it apart and put it back together again. And again. And again.

He'd come to Australia to do electrical engineering at university but then had dropped out. Bummed around for a while before he'd seen an ad for the spy shop franchise. He'd persuaded his parents to put up the money. And business, so far, had been pretty good.

As the conversation burbled along, Hanley doing most of the talking, I kept waiting for the right opportunity.

And then it came.

"Of course, not everything's on the shelves," he said, lowering his voice. "Got some stuff that's not strictly kosher, if you get my drift?"

I totally got his drift, but I still wasn't sure of a subtle way to bring up the IMSI-catcher.

"You wouldn't have an IMSI-catcher, would you?" I blurted.

Which was about as un as subtle can get, but it worked.

"Funny you should say that," he said, lowering his voice even further.

He walked over to the entrance, locked the door and flipped the card to *CLOSED*.

And then he told me about the IMSI-catcher, the one that he had built!

"Seriously, you built it?" I said.

"Why not?" he said. "I read on the net about this guy in the States who'd built one, so I thought if he can, then why can't I? Just because I don't have a uni degree doesn't mean I'm an idiot."

"So it's finished?"

"All ready to go," he said and I could hear the pride in his voice.

"You want somebody to test it for you?"

It had been going so well, I'd made the mistake of thinking that it would continue to go well.

He hit me with the obvious question: "What do you want an IMSI-catcher for?"

"Um," I said. "Ah," I said.

And then it came to me.

"There's this kid, right, by the name of Guzman, and he put some spyware on my phone, so I thought I'd show him a thing or two."

Hanley thought about this for a while, before he said, "You got it for tonight, but that's all."

He reached under the desk.

I was expecting something like I'd seen on the net, a neat black box with lights and meters.

But all he had in his hand was a cheap-looking flash drive. And an even cheaper-looking antenna.

"That's it?" I said.

"That's it," he said. "Load this software onto your laptop, plug this antenna into your USB and away you go."

PUTTING ME ON

All the way home I kept changing my mind: Hanley's putting me on, Hanley's not putting me on, Hanley's putting me on, Hanley's not putting me on.

And when I plugged the antenna in and stuck the flash drive into my laptop and nothing happened, not even the usual *drivers being installed*, I told myself that Hanley had been putting me on.

That he was probably telling somebody right now about this great joke he'd played on this kid. Bru.

But then I noticed it, on the side of the flash drive, a little switch thing – the flash drive was locked.

I flicked that and a message appeared on my computer: *drivers being installed*.

That went for a while and when it stopped a black screen appeared and a script ran. Then another one.

And another.

It was all very low-level, all very technical, and I didn't really have much idea what it was doing.

This stopped and I thought, *Is that it? But where's my IMSI-catcher?*

Again that thought: *Hanley's totally putting me on. Bru.*

A box popped up on my computer.

Enter target phone number

I entered the last of Guzman's numbers that Hound had given me.

More black boxes appeared, in which more low-level technical-looking scripts ran.

And then another box appeared: *Number successfully captured, phone currently being monitored.*

As if, I thought.

Because all I could hear was silence.

But then again, Guzman was a pretty unattractive unit and I doubted he'd have chicks calling him left, right and center.

He had to be communicating with somebody, though. A mother, an accountant, somebody.

Maybe it was a time thing. Maybe he was one of those stay-up-all-night-and-sleep-all-day nerds.

Or maybe Hanley was still putting me on, sitting in his shop having a huge Kiwi chuckle at my expense.

But then my laptop beeped and a box appeared on the screen.

Guzman was getting some communication, an incoming text!

It was from his very good friend Telstra offering Guzman a deal on some great new plans that were going to save him $$$.

Great, I thought.

But then another box appeared that said, *Target phone making outgoing call to following number: 31157550.*

A man with a Chinese accent answered Guzman's call with, "Yes."

Then Guzman's voice over my laptop's speaker: "Let's switch to IM."

Man with Chinese accent: "Network down."

Guzman: "Crap!"

Man with Chinese accent: "You too paranoid, Freddy Boy. Just talk. No problem."

Guzman hesitated before he said: "I need you to put some hardware together."

Man with Chinese accent: "What sort of hardware?"

Guzman: "You'll find out."

Man with Chinese accent: "No, I need to know now, or no work."

Again Guzman hesitated before he said, "Cerberus."

The Man with the Chinese accent emitted a low whistle before he said, "A hundred k."

Guzman: "That's ridiculous!"

Man with Chinese accent: "Ten k for the work and ninety k for my no talk."

Yet again Guzman hesitated, and for an excruciating second I thought he was going to hang up, but eventually he said, "Okay, it's a deal. I'll be there in half an hour."

Then he hung up.

Suddenly, with one tapped phone call, two worlds, the world of the Cerberus and the world of Guzman, had become one. Guzman was LoverOfLinux, and even though I'd had a hunch about it I still just couldn't get my head around that.

How had it happened?

Was it some sort of crazy, improbable coincidence?

But again I recalled that on the day we nabbed Nitmick I had the sense that he and Guzman knew each other well.

And I knew that Guzman frequented Cozzi's, so there was the Snake connection.

But how did it happen that something I just happened to find out when I was working for Hound later became the third installment of The Debt?

Could Hound be part of The Debt?

I didn't have time to think all this through right then, though, because I had to find out where they were meeting. And that clock was still ticking loudly.

I did the obvious thing: I called the same number

that Guzman had called.

The same person with the Chinese accent answered. "Yes."

Thinking quickly, I said, "I'd like to get some work done, please."

"Who are you?"

"Dominic," I said, but "Dominic" obviously wasn't good enough, because the phone immediately went dead.

I tried the number again but it didn't even ring – obviously my number was now blocked.

So how was I going to find the address?

No sooner had I asked myself that question than myself came up with the answer: reverse phone book.

I wasn't sure where I'd heard about them but I had.

And a quick google revealed that I hadn't been mistaken: there were quite a few sites offering reverse phone lookups in Australia.

I entered the number into one of them, hit enter, and got the following: *an address has been found for this number, please enter credit card details to unlock.*

Did everything today have to be difficult?

I'd used Dad's credit card many times before, always with his permission, but I didn't have time for such niceties today. So I just entered the details of his card, consented to a debit amount of $5.95 being made, and finally an address appeared on my screen: *Shop 4K, Electric Bazaar, Chinatown.*

I hit "print screen," shoved the resultant printout into my pocket.

After calling a taxi, I was about to exit when I thought of something: it's always good to have an alibi.

I picked up my broken iPhone 5 and put it in my pocket.

There was nobody downstairs except the chess pieces, arranged on the board, all ready to go.

But as I stood outside, yelling at the taxi for not being here, Tristan appeared again.

"Hey, where you going?" he said.

"Out," I said.

"Out where?"

"The Electric Bazaar," I said. "I need to get my iPhone repaired."

"That place is mad," said Tristan.

The taxi appeared and I raised my arm so he would know I was the fare.

"Okay if I tag along?" said Tristan.

Not okay, I thought. Not okay, I was about to say. But then I thought, why not? It would make my alibi stronger – *But Officer, I was off to get my iPhone fixed with my mate.* And I couldn't imagine Guzman, with his sparrow bones, being dangerous, that Tristan would be in any danger, at all.

"I guess so," I said. "If your olds are okay with it."

"They're okay with it," he said. "Why wouldn't they be?"

Why wouldn't they? *Well, maybe because the last time we went out together you got shot at, which caused something to short circuit in your brain, which caused you to steal, and then crash a Maserati, thereby putting you in a coma.*

"Get in," I said, opening the taxi's passenger door for him.

BIZARRE ELECTRIC

The Electric Bazaar was a six-story building right in the middle of Chinatown, a rambling rabbit warren of a place, full of escalators and corridors and hole-in-the-wall shops.

The sort of place you'd go to buy a dongle for your laptop, some counterfeit software, or to get a Cerberus assembled.

"You sure you don't want to go back?" I asked Tristan as we entered.

"No way," he said. "This is mega-exciting!"

The Debt was sort of the reason Tristan had ended up in a coma, so I was starting to feel guilty – mega-guilty – involving him in it again.

But I figured I might also need him around and not just for an alibi.

Because now that I was here I realized that I had absolutely no plan, no idea how I was going to get the Cerberus from Guzman.

I wasn't even sure I'd come to the right place.

As the scam with the couriers proved, Guzman was clever, very clever, and I wouldn't have been surprised if he'd fed me a whole lot of false clues, if I hadn't been eating a lot of red herrings lately.

The first thing I had to do was ascertain whether this address actually existed.

I assumed that shop 4K would be on the fourth floor, so we took a series of clunking escalators to that level.

But none of the shops – if you could call them that – seemed to be numbered 4K, so I decided to ask around.

The first person I approached didn't know where it was.

"You want to buy DVDs?" he said. "Best quality."

Neither did the second person.

"You want to buy software?" he said. "Special price for you."

I was starting to think that Guzman had indeed sent me on a wild-goose chase, but the third person I asked said, "I can do better price."

"Better price than what?" I said.

"Better price than 4K."

So it did exist.

"Okay," I said. "I'll get a quote from 4K and then I'll come and see you."

"I do better price," said the man.

"Just one thing," I said. "Where exactly is 4K?"

"In basement," said the man. "Dirty place, many cockroach."

We left the man and his better price and got in the crowded elevator.

It whirred and it groaned but eventually it started moving downwards.

Past floor 3. Past floor 2. But at the ground floor it stopped. The doors clanked open and Guzman was standing there.

Guzman and his muscle-for-rent, the man with the red bandana, who was holding a black attaché case.

Guzman looked at me and I looked at Guzman.

And my mind immediately went into who-knows-what? mode.

I knew that Guzman was here to get the Cerberus assembled.

But he didn't necessarily know that I knew that.

I knew that Guzman had arranged the courier scam.

But he didn't necessarily know that I knew that.

So it seemed to me that somehow I was in a position of power here, because I knew more stuff than he knew.

And my intuition told me that I had to keep it that way, bring it down to his non-knowing level.

No saying, "Aha, I know why you're here, Guzman!" or "You swiped my stuff, you scumbag!" – none of that.

Instead I brought my alibi, my broken iPhone, out of my pocket and said, "You wouldn't know where I could get this bad boy fixed, would you, Guzman?"

As he stepped into the elevator, Red Bandana following, Guzman looked at me, then at the phone, an "Ouch!" look appearing on his face.

"This floor," he said. "Right at the back. Ask for Nguyen."

"Okay, thanks," I said, taking Tristan by the elbow and guiding him out of the elevator.

"Who was that?" said Tristan as the doors jerked shut and the elevator continued on its way.

"That's the guy who pulled the stunt with the courier," I said.

"And you just let him go?" said Tristan, clenching his fists.

I imagined a UFC match, Tristan and Guzman in the Octagon. A knee in the Guzman's knurries, over and over. A punch deep in his guts, over and over.

It was a nice thought, but it wasn't going to happen, and it wasn't going to work.

Violence, not even the UFC-sanctioned type, wasn't going to get the Cerberus, wasn't going to pay this installment.

"That other dude, the one in the try-hard bandana, he looked sort of familiar," said Tristan.

"Yeah, he gets around," I said.

"So what now, squire?" said Tristan.

I was asking myself exactly the same question, but without the really quite annoying "squire" reference.

"We wait," I said.

"Okay," said Tristan. "We wait."

While we waited, hiding behind some potted palms, Tristan asked me questions, question upon question upon question, like a four-year-old kid in their why-is-the-sky-blue? phase.

Why did he arrange for the couriers?

What was he after?

Why didn't I just tell the cops?

My answers, quite creative in the beginning, became less and less so, until eventually I had no choice but to say, "Tristan, you really need to play the quiet game now."

"Just one more thing," he said.

"Okay, just one more."

"That dude with the try-hard bandana," he said. "I'm sure I've seen him somewhere before."

"Maybe on some eighties TV show," I joked, but Tristan was having none of this.

"I'm sure I've seen him," he said again.

Finally the elevator stopped, the doors slid open, and Guzman and Red Bandana, still holding the black attaché case, were standing there.

I still didn't have a plan except: keep out of their sight, follow them, wait for some sort of opportunity to present itself.

Tristan took a couple of steps forward, out of the cover of the potted palms.

"Get back!" I hissed.

"He's the scumbag that shot at me!" said Tristan, and he started running.

Guzman and Red Bandana were making for the door but Tristan was behind them, rapidly catching up.

His brain may have been rearranged but he'd lost none of his athletic prowess.

When he was a couple of meters away he yelled, "Hey, you!"

Both Guzman and Red Bandana stopped and looked around.

"You so shot at me!" said Tristan, and he launched himself at Red Bandana.

I'm sure there was time for Red Bandana to get out of the way, but he just stood there, sort of mesmerized, as Tristan smashed into him.

Both he and Tristan toppled to the floor.

As they did, Red Bandana lost grip of the black attaché case and it slid along the floor, coming to rest at the feet of a security guard.

By this time Tristan was on top of Red Bandana, pummeling him with his fists.

"You shot at me!" he kept saying. "You shot at me."

By this time I was out of the cover of the potted palms.

By this time Guzman was looking straight at me.

My first thought was: *the black attaché case, I have to get it before he does.*

But when I looked at Guzman I could see that his eyes were not on the attaché case, his eyes were on the exit.

Then it occurred to me: the black attaché case is a decoy.

So when Guzman started running for the exit, I ran after him.

Past the three security guards who were now trying to separate the pummeling Tristan from the pummeled Red Bandana, following Guzman onto the footpath.

This was a busy street at a busy time of the day and there were people everywhere.

Guzman was surprisingly fast, surprisingly agile, as he weaved through the crowd.

I was gaining on him, though.

In fact, I slowed down a bit.

Because I still didn't have a plan.

Because I couldn't imagine taking the Cerberus from Guzman against his will. I couldn't imagine tackling him, or hitting him. Not in broad daylight.

Eventually Guzman slowed down to a jog.

Then a walk.

He stopped.

Face red, chest heaving: he was suffering, and now was the perfect time to take him out.

"You idiot," he gasped. "You fell for it!"

"Fell for what?"

"The oldest trick in the book," he said. "Do you really think I've got it?"

I thought of the black attaché case, how easy it would've been for me just to scoop it up.

Was Guzman really that clever?

Had I really fallen for the oldest trick in the book?

Yes, he really was that clever but something, a sixth sense, an intuition, told me that he had the phone.

But how to get it off him?

It seemed to me that violence was the only way.

There were fewer people around here and the Gold Coast was famously where people didn't like to get involved.

But I couldn't do it. I couldn't king-hit Guzman. Or crash-tackle him the way Tristan had crash-tackled Red Bandana.

I'm sure Guzman could sense my reluctance because his eyes were now darting all over the place, searching for an escape route.

No, violence wasn't my thing. Not like it was Hound's thing.

But as soon as I had that thought I had another contradictory one.

Was violence really Hound's thing? Yes, he'd

caused my head to have its own ringtone, and yes, he was one scary-looking hombre, but I'd never seen him actually hurt anybody.

It wasn't violence that made him so formidable, it was the threat of violence.

Armed with that insight, I took a step towards Guzman. Drawing myself up to my full Hound-like height, I dropped my voice to what I hoped was a Hound-like growl and said, "Give me the Cerberus, Guzman!"

He took a step back, but not before I saw fear in his eyes.

"Give it to me now or I'll break every little birdie bone in your little birdie body," I said.

Guzman winced, and his hand went into his pocket and came out with the Cerberus.

Gleaming under the light, it looked so beautiful – tomorrow's technology, the most desirable piece of technology in the world.

I remembered what Miranda had said: was it a phone, or an encryption device, or some sort of sensing apparatus?

It seemed that it could be all of these and much more.

I took the phone from Guzman, and I took off. But as I did, it occurred to me: hadn't that been a bit too easy?

Why hadn't he put up more of a fight?

And when I heard him say, "You're an idiot if you really think they're going to let you keep that," I had the feeling, once again, that Guzman had put one over me, that he'd written my part for me and I'd played it exactly as he'd intended.

And as I ran I wondered if his "they" could possibly be the same "they" as my "they": The Debt.

No, that didn't make sense. But if "they" weren't The Debt, what "they" were they?

BRAIN REARRANGED

Keep going, I told myself as I hurried back past Electric Bazaar, the Cerberus clutched to my chest. *Tristan will be okay, just keep going.*

But obviously this message didn't get to where it needed to go because I didn't keep going.

My feet, my legs, my whatevers, took me back into Electric Bazaar.

Where Tristan was so not okay.

He was handcuffed, as was Red Bandana, and they were surrounded by police officers.

I knew I shouldn't have shown my face here, but just as I was about to un-show it Tristan saw me.

"That's him!" he yelled, trying to point – not that easy when you're handcuffed. "That's who I was with when this guy shot at me."

One of the police officers cocked a finger at me. *Come here, laddie.*

235

I contemplated running, but quickly decided against turning myself into target practice.

I'd had my chance to get away and I'd blown it. Now I'd have to deal with the consequences.

"Yes?" I said as I approached the policewoman.

"What's your name?" she said.

As I told her my name I noticed the Taser on her hip.

"How do you spell your surname?" she said, jotting in a little notebook with the stub of a pencil.

I told her how to spell my surname.

"So you know Tristan?" she said.

"He was there when this man tried to shoot me," said Tristan.

Red Bandana was standing with arms across his chest, lips pressed tight, eyes focused on the ceiling, obviously in total I'm-not-saying-anything, I-want-my-lawyer mode.

"And where was this?" said the policewoman.

"Reverie Island," said Tristan. "My parents have got a house there."

The policewoman jotted this down in her little notebook as well.

"And can you confirm this, Dominic?" she asked. "Can you confirm that you were shot at by this gentleman?"

This might be it, I thought. The point when Tristan got better again.

All I had to do was say, "Yes."

The policewoman repeated her question.

If I said "Yes" I knew what would happen: we'd all go down to the police station and there'd be statements and all sorts of crap we'd have to do.

It was already midday and I had to get the Cerberus to Anna's birthday party.

"You know what?" I said, taking my poor broken phone from my pocket. "I just came here to get my iPhone fixed."

"That's not a pretty sight," said the policewoman. "So you don't know Tristan here?"

"Sure I know him. We go to the same school. But nobody ever shot at us."

The facsimile of a smile on Red Bandana's face: he knew he was free now.

"Okay, then," said the policewoman. "You better go get that phone seen to. We'll sort this mess out."

I didn't want to look at Tristan, but I couldn't help myself.

His face, once only capable of a single expression – the smirk – was now capable of a whole range of emotions.

Like hurt. And hurt. And more hurt.

"I'm sorry," I mouthed, before I hurried away.

I hadn't gotten very far when I heard a scuffle behind me. I turned around to see Tristan launch himself, once again, at Red Bandana and the policewoman take out her Taser and zap Tristan. Immediately he dropped to the ground.

My first thought was: *she's killed him!*

But then the other policeman helped a stunned Tristan back to his feet.

I noticed the policewoman was now looking in my direction. I couldn't get involved; I took off again.

JUJITSU

"You having a good day?" asked Luiz Antonio.

I'd decided that the best, and safest, way to get to the café was with somebody I trusted.

And who did I trust?

Not many people, but Luiz Antonio was one of them.

And he came with a taxi.

"Amazing," I said.

"Good for you, amigo," said Luiz Antonio.

"Hey, can we listen to that music, you know, the bad head and sick feet song?" I asked as we headed towards the city.

"*Sim*," said Luiz Antonio, punching some buttons on the car stereo.

The song started.

Luiz sang along to it, and once again I was surprised at how tuneful his gravelly voice was.

I provided some accompanying percussion, thrumming the dashboard with my fingers.

"Seems like we have some company," said Luiz Antonio.

That's a strange lyric, I thought until I realized what he was talking about: alongside us was Hound's Hummer.

The passenger's window was down, and one of the Lazarus brothers was making a *pull over* gesture.

"You know them?" said Luiz Antonio.

"Unfortunately, yes," I said.

"And you want me to pull over?"

"Not really," I said. "Can you lose them?"

Luiz Antonio jammed his foot down and the taxi responded by backfiring twice. Apart from that, however, it chugged along at pretty much the same pathetic speed.

Losing them wasn't going to be much of an option.

I looked across at the Hummer.

The Lazarus now had a gun in his hands, a big one. And it was pointed at us.

"Maybe we better do what he said," I said.

Luiz Antonio turned into a disused parking lot, the Hummer on our tail. The broken concrete was tufted with grass. There were festering piles of rubbish. And the burned-out shell of a car.

We stopped. So did they. We got out. So did they.

So far, so B-grade Hollywood action movie.

Even the gun that the Lazarus had trained on us looked a bit like a prop.

I was sure it wasn't, though.

Hound brought out his wallet, extracted a twenty-dollar bill, waved it at Luiz Antonio and said, "Here's your fare, driver. Keep the change and get out of here."

Luiz Antonio didn't move, just looked at Hound's money as if it was a particularly ripe piece of doggy doo that he'd just stepped on.

"I never leave a customer anywhere unless they want me to," he said, turning to me.

I shook my head. *Don't leave me.*

"You hear what my man Hound said?" said Lazarus, poking the gun in Luiz Antonio's direction.

"I did," said Luiz Antonio. "But you obviously didn't hear what I said."

"Keep the gun on him," said Hound, turning his attention to me.

He started patting his pockets as if he was missing something.

"Oh no!" he said. "Forgot my phone. Tell you what, let me borrow yours."

"Sure," I said, taking out my old iPhone, holding it out.

Now it was Hound who had the doggy doo look on his face.

"You know what they call somebody like me, Youngblood? An 'early adopter.' My first mobile phone was so big I got a sore arm from using it. So you think somebody like me is going to be happy using old technology like that?"

How does he know? I wondered. But not for long. Of course he knew. He'd known all along.

He'd just let me do all the hard work, all the heavy lifting.

Hot on the heels of this realization came another one: Hound had nothing at all to do with The Debt, of course he didn't.

Because they, The Debt, had found out about the Cerberus at exactly the same time as I had. Zoe had been right: I was so owned, so bugged.

But right then wasn't the time to consider the implications of this, because Hound and his Lazarus and his gun were going to take my Cerberus.

I could run for it, I thought.

And I had no doubt that I could outrun both Hound and Lazarus. They had lots of muscles but not runner's muscles.

But a speeding bullet?

Superman I wasn't.

Besides, it wasn't just me: there was Luiz Antonio to think of as well.

What choice did I have?

I took out the Cerberus, held it out on my palm.

Gleaming under the Gold Coast sun, it looked so beautiful – tomorrow's technology, the most desirable piece of technology in the world.

Both Hound and Lazarus moved towards it.

Hound went to grab it, but in what was almost a reflex motion my arm jerked back.

"Give it to him," said Lazarus, aiming the gun directly at me, at my heart.

Luiz Antonio stepped in front of me.

What's he doing? He's going to get himself killed.

"Get out of my way!" barked Lazarus.

Get out of his way.

Luiz Antonio moved slowly and purposefully towards Lazarus, towards the gun.

In a move straight out of UFC, he suddenly dropped to his haunches, while sweeping out his leg and hooking it around Lazarus's calf.

Lazarus fell and the gun clattered to the ground.

Luiz Antonio picked up the gun.

It happened so quickly, so unexpectedly, I'm sure we were all – except for Luiz Antonio – in shock.

Hound was the first to recover.

"Now old-timer," he said, his voice soft, reassuring, "what say you give me the gun before somebody gets hurt?"

Both hands on the barrel, Luiz Antonio brought the gun down hard on the ground, snapping it in half.

He tossed the two pieces into a pile of rubbish.

Hound and Lazarus, who was now back on his feet, exchanged looks: *what an idiot.*

I tended to agree.

Lazarus moved towards Luiz Antonio, shaping up like a boxer, fists held high.

He tried a couple of jabs.

Head weaving, Luiz Antonio easily avoided them.

And then he slipped through the other man's guard, moving in close, bringing his knee into Lazarus's groin.

There were a few sounds: the first was of hard bone against soft flesh, the second was a *whoosh* sound as the air was expelled from Lazarus's body, the third was Lazarus collapsing onto the concrete, and the final sound was harder to describe: it was a cross between a scream and a moan, maybe we should call it a scroam, but whatever it was, it was the most terrible sound I'd ever heard come out of another human being.

Hound looked at the pile of scroaming Lazarus and then at the man responsible for it.

"So you know a bit of kung fu, do you?" he said.

"Brazilian jujitsu," said Luiz Antonio. "It's called Brazilian jujitsu."

I could see Hound's hand reaching for his side.

"Watch out!" I said. "He's going for his Mace."

Luiz Antonio danced into action again.

A spin, a kick, and Hound, too, was kissing concrete.

Ω   Ω   Ω

On the way to the café I didn't say anything. I couldn't say anything. There was too much to digest.

Eventually, when we pulled up outside, I found some words.

"Who are you?"

Luiz Antonio indicated the taxi license, the one where he looked like he was in that cheesy band my mum likes, the Eagles.

"No, who are you really?" I asked.

"Just a taxi driver who likes to make sure his customers get to their destinations."

As far as explanations went, it was hardly adequate.

Right then, it'd do, though.

I had other things to think about – like how to get to a party I hadn't been invited to, at a time and place I didn't know.

SPARTEE

The line at Latte Day Saints was even longer, snaking even further down the street. I followed my mother's example and pushed my way inside and into a wall of khaki.

I looked up, at yet another security guard.

"We have a line," said this particular one.

"Is the owner here?" I asked.

The security guard didn't answer.

"Can you tell him that Dom, the son of Celia Silvagni, would like to have a quick word with him?"

The security guard considered my request before he said, "No, I can't. Now if you could please join the end of the line."

Look, I'm not one of those street kids like Brandon who hates security guards, who sees them as their natural enemy, who spends all day plotting their downfall.

But this one was being pretty unreasonable.

So when I saw Simon appear from the back of the café, that teeth-whitening-ad smile on his face, I used my athlete's reflexes to dodge past the unreasonable wall of unreasonable khaki.

"Hi," I said as I approached Simon. "Do you remember me?"

The blank look on his face suggested that he didn't, so I gave him some help. "I'm Dom, Celia Silvagni's son."

By this time all that khaki had reached us.

"Sorry, boss," he said. "He sneaked past."

"It's okay, Sam. I'll deal with it," Simon said.

The security guard moved off.

"How is your wonderful mother?" said Simon, the smile increasing in intensity.

"I was here with her about a week ago," I said.

"That's right," he said. "And didn't she look just wonderful?"

"Wonderful," I said. "And there was this girl Anna at the next table. She was here with her parents. Do you remember her?"

"We get a lot of people through here," he said, looking over my shoulder.

"She was fifteen and she was really beautiful but sort of skinny, too," I said.

"Like I said, a lot of people."

"And her parents, they …" I started, trying to remember exactly what her parents looked like.

When her father stood up to pay the bill, he was quite tall, I remembered that. And he'd had close-cropped hair.

And then I saw it, in Anna's father's hand.

"He paid with a credit card!" I said.

"Yes, quite a few of our customers choose the convenience of a card," said Simon.

"But you'd have a record," I said. "You'd have a record of his name!"

The smile was still there, but the intensity was waning rapidly.

"That is not information I'm permitted to share," he said, making a *come here* signal to the security guard.

"Do you know I could tweet right now saying I saw a cockroach in your coffee grinder and I guarantee you by the morning it would be on thousands of other tweets and furthermore just about everybody who read it would believe it?"

There was no smile now, just two lips pressed together to form a very thin, very straight line.

"What day was it again?" he said, waving the security guard away.

"Last Saturday."

"And the time?"

"Around eleven," I said.

"Wait here," he said.

He disappeared in the back, returning a few minutes later.

"Russo," he said.

"R-u-s-s-o?" I said, spelling it out.

"That's right, Russo."

I thanked him and left.

There must be a lot of girls called Anna Russo in the world, I thought. But what did I know about my Anna Russo?

I knew that she was fifteen, or sixteen, depending on the actual date of her birthday.

I knew that she lived on the Gold Coast.

And I knew she wanted a Cerberus. I knew that she liked technology.

I took out my phone.

Got online.

Went to Facebook.

Went to *Search for People*, and entered *Anna Russo*.

Hit return.

There were *over 500 results*, Facebook's way of saying it had given up even counting.

I entered *Australia* into the country field and hit *Refine search*.

Now there were forty-two results.

I started scrolling through these, studying each photo intently.

And I soon realized that I had a problem: not everyone used their real photo in their profile.

So my Anna Russo might be a fluffy cat, or a bunch of daffodils, or even a well-known supermodel.

I kept going, though; what choice did I have?

The twenty-second Anna Russo looked like she was about two years old.

There was something about her, though.

I went to her Facebook page.

Anna only shares some of her Profile information with everyone, it said.

Wow. Pretty selective for a two year old.

But I could see her friends.

All three hundred and twelve of them!

What two year old has three hundred and twelve friends?

I started looking through them. Mostly they were teenagers. Mostly they were girls.

When I came to Ava Kiviat I stopped.

There was a Brett Kiviat at my school, this brainiac kid who was part of the library pond life. And Kiviat wasn't a very common name.

Brett Kiviat was a friend of Cooper Nielson.

Who lived in the same street as Rashid.

I called Rashid.

He answered straightaway.

"They going to let you run?"

"Apparently not," I said.

"Then, as protest, I'm not going to run, too."

"Don't be crazy, Rashid. You run. You have to!" I said. "You wouldn't have Cooper Nielson's number, would you?"

"Yeah," he said. "What do you want to talk to him for?"

"Just text it to me, okay? I'll explain later."

I hung up, and the message arrived a couple of seconds later.

I called Cooper Nielson's number.

He didn't answer.

So I left a message: "Hi, I know you're going think this is weird but it's Dom Silvagni here. You know, from school. Rashid's friend. Anyway, I really need to talk to you, so if you could call me back as soon as possible, that'd be really great."

Five minutes later my phone rang.

It was Cooper Neilson.

Yes, he did think it was weird.

But yes, he had Brett Kiviat's number.

"Thanks so much," I said.

"You know it's in the White Pages?" he said.

"The White Pages?"

"Yeah, it's this book that's got people's phone numbers in it. It's also online."

"Oh, those White Pages."

I hung up and waited for Brett Kiviat's number to arrive.

When it did, I called it.

And got a message: *This phone is turned off or out of range.*

Then I remembered what Cooper Nielson had said.

Went to the Gold Coast White Pages Online. Typed *Kiviat* into the search field and hit enter.

I got two hits, two landline numbers. I called the first one.

A man answered. "Hello."

"Hello, my name is Dom Silvagni and I'm after Brett Kiviat. I'm not sure if I have the right number."

"You have," said the man. "I'm his father, but Brett's at a chess tournament this weekend."

"Oh," I said, my brain in overdrive now. "Actually, is Ava there? She might be able to help me."

"Ava's at a birthday party."

"Anna Russo's party, right?" I said, trying to contain my excitement.

"Yes, that's right," he said, and I almost fainted. Haystack. Needle. You get the picture.

"So it's at her place?"

"Oh no," said the father. "They're having it at that flash new place in the city."

"Flash new place in the city" didn't help me that much.

"The new McDonald's?" I said.

"No, it's that one that looks like they should be growing tomatoes inside it."

"The glass cube, you mean? The Styxx Emporium?"

"That's it," he said, and by the time I'd hung up I was already out on the road hailing a taxi.

I couldn't help smiling as I rushed into the glass cube imagining rows of trellised tomato plants, plump red tomatoes hanging underneath.

I skipped down the glass staircase and realized the place was even more crowded than usual.

Every staff member, every Styxx Knowledge Consultant, was surrounded by people.

When they moved, the customers moved too, like an orbiting planet with its many moons.

This is no time for politeness, I told myself as I approached the nearest constellation.

"Excuse me," I said, surprised at how loud and assertive my voice sounded. "Can you tell me where the birthday party is today?"

I got several glares and one muttered comment – "Nice manners, not!" – but I did get an answer from the Styxx Knowledge Consultant: "Downstairs, it's on your invite."

"Oh, I left my invite at home," I said.

"Then you can't get in," she said, turning her attention back to her moons.

First I tried the elevator.

When I got in, I pressed the Lower Floor button, but it didn't illuminate.

I remembered the last time I was here, when I was taken downstairs for an interview, how the woman

253

had swiped her security card.

It was the stairs, then.

There was not one, but two Styxx Knowledge Consultants standing at the top of the stairs. And one of them was holding some sort of portable scanning device in one hand and a clutch of invitations in the other.

Pretending that they were not there, I went to take the first step, but of course one of them said, "Excuse me, this is restricted access."

"I'm late for the party," I said. "Anna Russo's party."

"Invite?" he said.

"I left it at home."

"It clearly states on the invite that you will need it in order to attend the party."

"I know that, but this friend of mine, Tristan, he was in a coma so I had to visit him in the hospital. And you know, I just forgot it. And Anna and me, we're, like, the oldest friends you could imagine."

The two Knowledge Consultants exchanged looks.

"Do you have an invite or not?" one of them asked.

"Not," I said.

I could've made a dash for it, but I could see that at the bottom of the stairs there was another security door.

Making a dash for it wasn't going to get me very far.

It was so frustrating: I knew she was down there, maybe even under my feet, and I could feel the Cerberus in my pocket.

Cerberus.

Of course!

Ignoring the line, I charged up to the nearest counter.

"Cerberus," I said. "I'd like to buy a Cerberus."

The consultant had already taken a step back from the counter. A manager soon arrived – fortunately not the same manager as before – and asked me to accompany him.

It was the same deal as before: into the elevator, the manager swiping his card, and us traveling down to the Lower Floor.

As we got out, I ran for it.

Down the corridor, doors on either side.

Manager's Office. Assistant Manager's Office.

Function Room.

I tried the door handle.

It was unlocked.

Pushed the door open.

The sPartee was in full swing, the room full of sPartee facilitators, of parents, of kids.

I recognized three people: Anna, her father and her mother.

But nobody recognized me.

"This is a private party," an older man said.

Somebody said something to him in a foreign language, a language that sounded like Italian, or maybe even Calabrian.

"He went in there!" came a voice from up the hall.

Now they were all looking at me, everybody in the room.

"I just brought a present for Anna," I said, my hand reaching into my pocket.

Anna's father stepped in front of Anna, as if to say, *You're not going anywhere near my daughter.*

But Anna stepped around her father, walked towards me, hand out.

We met in the middle of the room and I gave her the present.

She looked at it and then at me. "It's the real deal?"

"The real deal," I said, though I actually wasn't sure if it was or not.

On the way here, in the taxi, I'd tried to turn it on but hadn't been able to.

Thumb flying, Anna pressed a combination of buttons and the screen flickered to life.

And that's pretty much when it all – all sHell – broke loose.

Because Anna took off, headed for the back door.

She was surprisingly fast and everybody, including me, took a while to react.

If she's out of here, so am I, I thought, following her.

"Grab that kid!" somebody yelled.

Security guards rushed over and tried to do just that.

But I was able to fend them off and follow Anna through the back door, slamming it shut behind me.

Down another corridor I followed her, until we reached a door that said *Fire Escape Only Use in Case of Emergency*.

"What now?" I said, but Anna had already answered my question: she cracked the door open and a siren blasted. And then another one. And another one.

We ran up the stairs. One flight. Two flights. And there were no more stairs. Just a door.

I tried the handle. It was unlocked.

"But what's on the other side?" I said, thinking of cops, security guards.

"Got no choice," said Anna, her breath ragged.

There was volley of footsteps behind us, getting louder, getting closer.

She was right: we didn't have much choice.

I pushed down the handle, flung open the door, and it was an alley.

It was dirty, it was dingy, it was about as far removed from a dazzling glass cube as you could get, but to me it truly was an architectural masterpiece, one of the most beautifully designed places I'd ever seen.

It was our way out.

"This way!" I said, indicating left.

"Good luck," said Anna as she moved to the right.

Who was she?

But I wasn't going to find out, not now anyway.

More footsteps from behind, voices too: there was no time to lose.

"You, too," I said, and I ran left and down the alley and onto a busy street.

As I kept running, I felt an increasing sense of exhilaration.

I felt like a Superman who was not fazed by kryptonite.

A Hulk without the anger-management issues.

A Batman who didn't need the Boy Wonder.

I felt like I was capable of anything.

Capture the Zolt? Tick.

Turn off the city's lights? Tick.

Get a Cerberus?

I'd done exactly what they'd asked me to do: I'd repaid the third installment.

Another great big beautiful tick for me.

LOOPHOLE

"Isn't it this just so exciting?" said Mom at the dinner table, her head swiveling from Gus, to Dad, to Miranda, to me. "Imagine when he wins!"

She had just gotten off the phone with Toby.

All the contestants were staying in a big house in some sort of pre-final lockup before the final itself was taped tomorrow.

"Yes, it's exciting," we all agreed.

Almost as soon as I'd arrived home, the wave of exhilaration I'd surfed all the way from the Styxx Emporium had died.

In surfer talk, it had gone from gnarly to onshore slop.

And now all I felt was this aching sadness in my gut.

Yes, I'd repaid the third installment.

But tomorrow there was a race and I wasn't in it.

A race that I'd trained all year, all my life for, and I wasn't in it.

If I'd been injured, or if I hadn't been good enough, then I would've taken it on the chin.

But I wasn't injured.

And I was good enough: I'd qualified fair and square.

Or was this the real debt? Maybe all the repayments: the Zolt, the lights, the Cerberus, they were nothing. Maybe what they really wanted from me was the thing I loved most in the world, maybe what they wanted was my running.

Okay, maybe it was my fault because I didn't think through the get-suspended-from-school thing.

But before The Debt, I'd never had the need, or the urge, to ditch school. Never.

"You better get your brand ready," I'd said to Dad, almost skipping, as soon as I got home.

"Just don't get too full of yourself," had been his reply.

After that I'd gone across to Gus's house and told him the news, the first time I'd spoken to my grandfather since I'd yelled at him in the morning.

He hadn't said anything, just wrapped his bony arms around me and squeezed. Because of all those weights he lifted, a Gus squeeze was something to be reckoned with.

"Steady," I said, squirming. "You're going to break my ribs."

Mum served the pasta but, despite what I'd been through, I just wasn't hungry.

"Did you hear that they had to evacuate the Styxx Emporium today? Some sort of fire alarm went off," said Miranda.

Okay, she didn't exactly look at me when she said this, but I wondered how much my sister knew. She was smart, Miranda. More than smart. She must've known that something was going on, especially after all those Styxx-related questions I'd asked her.

"They had to close the street off," said Dad. "The traffic was absolute chaos."

The intercom buzzed.

"Who could that be at this time?" Mom said.

Dad picked up the handset.

"Yes, Samsoni," he said. "Yes. Of course. Can you just hold on?"

He put his hand over the mouthpiece. "A Mr. Ryan's at the gate. He says he's from the boys' school."

"He's the civics teacher," Mom said, looking at her watch. "What's he doing here at this time of the night on the weekend?"

"He says he has something very important to tell us," said Dad.

"But we're eating," said Mom.

Without any further consultation Dad said into

the mouthpiece, "Send Mr. Ryan up, Samsoni."

It was obvious that Mom was pretty annoyed but she didn't say anything.

A couple of minutes later and Mr. Ryan, dressed in his usual chinos and blue cotton shirt, a satchel in his hand, walked through our front door.

"I'm terribly sorry to intrude," he said, "but I have some news I thought was better delivered in person. I've been doing a little light reading." He opened his satchel.

"*Regulations of the Schools Athletics Board*," he said, extracting a thick white book. "Look, some of the stuff in here is pretty legalistic, but I'll put it in simple terms: basically, they can't stop Dom from running tomorrow."

"They can't?" I said, my heart pulling at its mooring ropes, getting ready to soar.

"No, they can't," said Mr. Ryan. "Not according to their own regulations."

My heart broke free, soaring – they couldn't stop me from running!

"But we can," said Mom. "According to our regulations."

All eyes were now on her.

"I thank you very much for your concern, Mr. Ryan. And I appreciate you coming over. But Dom made a bad decision, actually quite a few bad decisions, and he has to live with the consequences of those decisions."

Mom walked over to the door, opened it.

Poor Mr. Ryan, he must've been so excited, and now he was being kicked out, humiliated.

And my soaring heart had crash-landed, Zolt-style.

I looked over at Gus, then Dad.

Something was going on between them, some sort of wordless conversation.

Just as Mr. Ryan was about to walk through the door Dad said, "Mr. Ryan, could you please hold on?"

Mr. Ryan stopped, looked back.

"Are you saying that if my son turns up tomorrow, they have to let him run?"

"Absolutely," said Mr. Ryan, throwing a nervous look at Mom. "And it's not as if anybody took his place, they were just going to run the race with one less competitor."

Dad looked at me and said, "And Dom, you want to run?"

I nodded. Yes, I want to run. More than anything in the world I want to run.

"Then Dom should run," said Dad.

Mom and Dad didn't do scenes.

Not public ones anyway.

So they disappeared outside while the rest of us stayed where we were.

But even from the dining room we could hear their raised voices.

The smashing of furniture.

A gunshot.

Not quite, but their debate did sound pretty vigorous.

Eventually they came back inside, and Dad was looking like he'd just done some serious time in the Octagon. "Looks like we're going to Sydney," he said, trying to keep the triumph out of his voice.

Mom rolled her eyes before she turned on the plasma.

"Where can I find the last episode of *Junior Ready! Set! Cook!*" she asked Miranda, resident media guru.

The four of us – Dad, Gus, Mr. Ryan and me – moved to the living room with Dad's laptop to try to find a way to get me to Sydney.

At first we were going to take a commercial flight in the morning, but we couldn't find any that would get us there in time to register. Not when you took into account the taxi trip from the airport to the stadium.

Then Dad said, "No problem, we'll charter a flight."

But there was an issue with that too.

There just weren't any charters available out of the Gold Coast.

Dad was in the middle of contacting a friend of his, to see if he could borrow his jet, when Gus said, "Dave, why don't we just take the bloody car?"

"But it's a twelve-hour drive!" said Dad.

"Exactly," said Gus. "So let's hit the road now, otherwise Dom won't make it to the registration in time."

Dad put his phone down and said, "You're right, a big old road trip."

He looked at Mr. Ryan, then Gus, and then at me before he sighed and said, "I'll go and sort it with your mother."

It took him half an hour to sort it and even then I don't know how sorted it actually was, because when he came back he said, "Come on, let's get out of here."

There was no packing, none of that; I just grabbed my running gear and threw it into the back of Dad's Porsche 911.

"Well, thanks for your trouble," said a smiling Dad to Mr. Ryan, going to shake his hand as they both stood in our driveway.

"Are you joking?" said Mr. Ryan and the smile dropped from Dad's face.

"Do you think I'm going to miss a big old road trip?" said Mr. Ryan. "Besides, you need somebody at the other end to deal with any legal issues."

So Dad drove, Mr. Ryan sat in the passenger seat, and Gus and I squeezed into the back.

When we saw the sign that said *Sydney 824 km*,

Dad let out a wild yell of joy.

It was so extraordinarily un-Dad-like that I was a bit embarrassed for him – and me – especially in front of Mr. Ryan.

And when my grandfather responded with a yell of his own, even louder than Dad's, my embarrassment increased exponentially.

"Calm down, guys," I wanted to say. "This is my civics teacher here."

But my civics teacher already had his mouth open and a noise was already coming out.

A noise so deranged, so unhinged, so loud it would have put any banshee to shame.

When the last reverberations had died away, Mr. Ryan's effort received a deserved round of applause.

"Dom, do you want to have a go?" said Dad.

"I might just preserve my energy for the race," I said.

And my dignity.

"Good idea," said Gus.

Dad's phone rang.

Nothing unusual there – Dad's phone was always ringing, it was perhaps the ringiest phone in the whole of Australia.

But instead of answering it like he always did, he did another extraordinary un-Dad-like-thing: he turned his phone off and then tossed it into the glove compartment.

"Okay, fellas," he said, holding out his hand.

"Let's have them."

Mr. Ryan was the first to relinquish his phone. And then Gus gave his over. My hand went into my pocket but I just couldn't do it.

"Dom?" said Dad, holding out his hand.

"Do I really have to?" I said. "Shouldn't at least one of us be online in case there's an emergency or something?"

But Dad's hand remained where it was, so I reluctantly took out my old iPhone 4, turned it off and gave it to him.

Dad put his foot down and I could feel myself being sucked back into my seat.

"Holy Moses!" said Mr. Ryan. "This thing's got some poke!"

"You want a turn later?" Dad asked him.

"Seriously?"

"Well, you don't think I'm going to do all the driving, do you?"

Dad fiddled around with his iPod until he found some Rolling Stones, apparently one of their earlier albums.

Personally I thought all their albums were earlier albums.

Mr. Ryan, it seemed, despite the identikit chinos and blue cotton shirt, was also a big fan of the Stones.

And while they discussed whether Keith Richards really did use an acoustic guitar on the opening riff of "Jumpin' Jack Flash," I felt my eyelids getting heavier.

"Stretch yourself out," Gus told me. "You need some shut-eye before the race."

It was a Porsche 911, I wanted to tell him, there wasn't really anywhere to stretch out.

Gus unclipped his prosthetic leg, shoved it under Dad's seat.

"That gives you a bit more leg room," he said, pressing his bony frame against the door.

I was still reluctant to take up more than my share of space.

"Come on, stick your head here," said Gus, patting his thigh.

I did as he said: curled up in the seat, rested my head on his thigh.

As far as pillows went, it wasn't even close. And the car was full of noise, the throaty roar of the Porsche's exhaust and the jagged chords of Keith's acoustic – or was it electric? – guitar.

The last thing I heard before I fell asleep was Gus humming the bad head, sick feet song.

FARTS UNFARTED

When I woke, the interior of the car was flooded with soft morning light. And it smelled like farts: old farts, new farts and farts yet to be farted.

Dad and Gus were slumbering and Mr. Ryan was driving. He must've been enjoying using up all that fossil fuel he'd saved by putting around in a Prius because the Porsche was flying, the needle twitching around the one-eighty kph mark.

"Morning," I said, sitting up, rubbing the sleep out of my eyes.

"Morning," said Mr. Ryan.

"It must've been some night," I said, noticing the McDonald's wrappers on the floor, the empty cans of Red Bull.

"It was," said Mr. Ryan, breaking into a huge smile. "Your dad –"

I waited for the next part of the statement, wondering what he was going to say: *your dad is an amazing driver, your dad is an astute businessman, your dad knows a lot about the Rolling Stones?*

"– he sure knows how to let one rip," he said.

"Look who's talking," said Dad, who obviously wasn't as asleep as I'd thought he was. "Old Trumpet Bum here. Old Organ Arse."

Gus opened his eyes and said, "You young fellows don't know the first thing about flatulence. In my day, we would've shredded the upholstery in this thing."

"You want to give us an example, Dad?" said Dad, winking at Mr. Ryan. "Show us what it was all about back in the day?"

"Them days are gone," said Gus, shaking his head. "And at my age you never trust a fart."

We stopped for fuel and Dad and Mr. Ryan changed places.

"Take the next exit," said Gus.

"GPS reckons it's the one after," said Dad.

"Bugger the GPS," said Gus. "You want to get the kid registered on time or not?

Dad took the next exit.

Gus gave directions, Dad drove like a maniac, but it seemed like all the traffic lights were conspiring against getting me registered.

We sat at one, engine ticking, traffic static.

"Stuff this," said Dad, looking both ways before he planted his foot, the Porsche taking off with a squeal of rubber.

"Wow!" I said.

Gus shook his head.

This was a Dad I hardly knew.

Another thought occurred to me: this is the Dad who repaid The Debt. Who spoke Calabrian.

Between buildings, I could now see glimpses of the Olympic Stadium's soaring walls.

Dad turned into the drive and pulled up outside the entrance. Even before we'd come to a complete stop Mr. Ryan was out of the door, *Regulations of the Schools Athletics Board* in his hand.

He raced for the entrance.

Despite the chinos, he showed plenty of speed, and you could see why he still held that school cross-country record.

We parked the Porsche in the parking lot. All three of us got out, hurried towards the entrance.

"No matter what happens," said Dad, "I'd just like to thank you guys for a great time."

"Bloody waste of effort if Dom doesn't run," said Gus.

In through the entrance, and I was getting excited: this was where the Kenyan Noah Ngeny had beaten the world record holder Hicham El Guerrouj in the final of the 1500 meters.

I was also getting worried: what if Mr. Ryan and his chinos had gotten it wrong?

As we neared the registration area I could see Mr. Ryan talking to a fluoro-jacketed official, pointing to something in the book.

She was a big official; there was a lot of fluoro.

Mr. Ryan saw me and beckoned with his hand: *Come here.*

I jogged over.

The official, whose name I could see from one of the many passes that hung around her neck was Marge Jenkins, gave me a once-over.

Wasn't she the one who got the Kenyans disqualified? I asked myself.

"Here's Dom," said Mr. Ryan. "As you can see, he's raring to go!"

I gave Ms. Jenkins my best raring-to-go look.

She glanced back down at the book and shook her head.

"Well, I suppose rules are rules," she said. "But, really, this is most irregular."

Mr. Ryan punched the air with his fist.

"I'm running!" I yelled, legs propelling me upwards, arms pumping. "I'm running in the nationals!"

THE NATIONALS

Despite how long it had taken to get here, I still couldn't quite believe that I was about to compete in the national championships.

I sort of expected somebody to snap their fingers and I'd be back in Halcyon Grove, about to watch Toby compete in the *Junior Ready! Set! Cook!* final.

I think this was why I didn't find the other competitors as threatening as I usually did.

Coach Sheeds got the three of us – me, Rashid and Bevan Milne – together for a pep talk.

It was a good one, too, and I could see that the others were suitably pepped, but I still felt pretty relaxed.

So relaxed that when I saw Seb on the side of the track peeling off his tracksuit I didn't really react that much, not like I should've.

Oh, Seb's here, I thought, and then my thoughts moved on to other things, like what a lovely day it was, how high the walls of the stadium were, and how amazing it must've been to be here when Cathy Freeman won gold in the 400 meters.

Even when Seb caught my eye and gave me a thumbs-up it still didn't occur to me how weird it was that he was here.

In fact, if Bevan Milne hadn't said, "What in the blazes is Seb doing competing?" I might not have reacted at all.

"Seb?" I said.

"Yes," said Bevan Milne. "Your mate Seb. He's down on the starting list."

"But who's he racing for?" I asked. "He doesn't even go to school."

"Well, he obviously found some loophole," said Bevan Milne.

"Obviously," I said, thinking that loopholes weren't such a bad thing, actually.

We took our positions on the starting line, the starter did his thing, and we were off.

It didn't take me long, maybe half a lap, to realize that I had absolutely no chance of winning the National Junior 1500 Meter title.

The Debt had totally trashed my preparation, the other runners were too strong.

But as weird as it sounds, I didn't even want to try to win this race.

Because if I did, if I went for broke, I knew I'd

blow up, I knew the other runners would mow me down like the grass at the Halcyon Grove Recreation Precinct and I'd struggle in a distant and dismal last.

I didn't want to try to medal either, to finish second or third.

No, I wanted to finish fourth.

Because fourth would be enough to get me on the team to compete in the World Youth Games in Rome.

As we entered the third lap, Rashid and I were running abreast, stride for stride, and Seb was hard on our heels.

The leaders, a tight bunch of four runners, were about twenty meters in front of us.

I was starting to hurt, the usual lap-three blues – burning thighs, oxygen getting hard to find – but as Coach Sheeds was fond of saying, *Pain is inevitable, suffering is optional, boys.*

By the start of the bell lap one runner had dropped off the leading bunch.

This was exactly what I'd been counting on: the occasion had gotten to somebody, they'd gone out too hard and were now paying the price.

The three of us moved past him, and there were now only three runners between us and the finish line.

I didn't care about them, they could divvy up the hardware between them; it was fourth I had my eyes on.

I took a quick glance behind; there was too much distance for the other runners to make up, they weren't in contention.

The last place was between Seb, Rashid and me.

I knew that I had a much bigger kick than they did, even if my training hadn't been optimal.

Both of them knew that I had a much bigger kick than they did, even if my training hadn't been optimal.

Really, if either was to have any chance, they needed to kick now.

I looked across at Rashid.

He smiled at me, a resigned smile.

He's not going to go, I thought. *He's given up on going to Rome.*

Well, there wasn't much I could do about that.

Up ahead the front runners had kicked, two of them pulling quickly away from the third.

There was over three hundred meters to go, and I thought of Coach Sheeds's instructions, which were exactly the same as Gus's instructions: "Kick with two hundred to go, not a millimeter more, not a millimeter less."

Up ahead the third runner had dropped back even more.

He's really struggling, I thought. *He's hit the wall.*

Suddenly it occurred to me: if we both pass him, then Rashid and I would both qualify.

But it's too far out to kick, I told myself. *What if I blow up, don't even make fourth?*

"Rashid," I puffed.

"What?"

"Come on, let's get him!"

I kicked.

Two-fifty meters out and I kicked.

I could almost hear both Coach Sheeds and Gus going, "Noooooo!"

Rashid went with me and Seb jumped into our slipstream.

The crowd, silent throughout the race, found its voice.

Now I could see why they called this place the Colosseum, now it felt like the sort of place where two men would fight to the death.

Fifty meters from the finish and we reeled the third runner in.

Coach Sheeds and Gus had gotten their math right, though – after kicking for two hundred meters, I hit the wall.

It was the three of us, Rashid, Seb and me, side by side, straining for the finish.

Seb powered ahead, and Rashid and I went stride for stride.

I was gone, nothing left.

But I thought of how I'd caught the Zolt, how I'd turned the lights off, how I'd gotten a Cerberus.

Finding something extra, I lunged for the tape, but it was no good, Rashid got his barrel chest millimeters ahead of me.

I was congratulating Seb, congratulating Rashid, when an official said, "Don't get too carried away, we're having a look at the photo."

For ten minutes we sat on the grass as the officials flitted about.

Then there was an announcement over the PA.

First the winner and the second-placed were announced.

"Coming in third," said the announcer, "is Sebastian Baresi."

Despite all the misgivings I had about him I couldn't help smiling at our pool guy. Loose as a goose on the juice. He'd run a clever race.

"And coming in fourth today, and also on his way to Rome for the World Youth Games, is Dominic Silvagni."

I rushed over to the officials' tent, to all the officials assembled there.

How could they have all gotten it wrong?

"Rashid was ahead of me!" I said.

"The camera does not lie," said Marge Jenkins.

"But –" I started, before I was interrupted by another official, a red-faced woman holding a phone.

"Dominic Silvagni?" she said.

"Yes."

"It's your mother."

I grabbed the phone.

"Mom, what's up?"

"None of you had your phones on," she said, her voice skittish, like a top on a smooth surface.

"Mom, what's wrong?"

"It's Toby," she said. "He's gone missing!"

"Missing?"

"From the *Ready! Set! Cook!* house. They went to wake him up this morning and he wasn't there. They can't find him anywhere!"

She said something else, but I wasn't really listening because all I could hear was Hound's voice, full of ice.

I reckon it would be really, really difficult to make ice cream if you had ten broken fingers. You know, with all that whisking they do.

It was too much to process: I wasn't going to Rome, I was going to Rome, Toby was missing.

Too much to process, so I didn't. I screwed my eyes tight, I jammed my thumbs into my ears, I dropped to the grass and I curled up into a ball.